LIFE'S OASIS

THE LOVE LEGACY
Book Two

A.F. VOYLES

aBM

Published by:

A Book's Mind

PO Box 272847

Fort Collins, CO 80527

www.abooksmind.com

Copyright © 2016

ISBN: 978-1-944255-24-4

Printed in the United States of America

My desire is that this series will bring hope to your heart and minister to your soul through creative writing and the inspiration of the Holy Spirit.

This book is dedicated to Nelda Nicole Voyles and Natalie Nasha Anderson, my two precious daughters. God graced me with your presence, and I am forever grateful. You both are jewels in the crown of my life. I am thankful for the privilege of being a part of your lives and the many lessons you taught me. Nicole, you may have left this earth on Sept. 12, 1992, but you are forever engraved in our hearts and memories as a priceless pearl. We will wrap our arms around you again one day in eternity's realm.

Thank you Melvin (Red) Voyles, my dearest companion and friend, for being my Rojomen. You always look out for me, protect, and take care of me. I could not ask for a better mate. You truly love me like Jesus loves His church.

Thank you to my family (blood born and blood bought). You know who you are! I love you all! Thank you for all the contributions, prayers, blood, sweat and tears you have made to my life.

Thank you Pastor Steve and Angel Ryan with Grace Life Church for believing in me when I didn't believe in myself.

Thank you to all the doctors out there who take the time to listen and care. Thank you Dr. Sara Edmund for your gentle and kind spirit. Thank you Oasis of Hope hospital and Dr. Contreras Jr.

Thank you to my publisher – Jenene Scott, A Book's Mind Team (Floyd), and editor – Christine Flower. Thank you to all the other authors out there whose input is priceless. Never give up on your dreams – see them through to fruition.

Thank you Jesus for the creative seed you planted in my spirit and soul; that you are growing on a daily basis and using for Your good and glory! Thank you for helping me to tell my story in this way. Nothing is impossible with You!

Oasis

A small fertile or green area in a desert region,
usually having a spring or well.
Something serving as a refuge, relief, or pleasant
change from what is usual, annoying, difficult, etc.
Psalms 91:2

Chapter One
A NEW HOME

Brian and Maria had no idea their exclusive mountain getaway would yield the buried dream of their hearts. The solitude of her parents' cabin enchanted the mind and lulled the soul to a restful place. The perfect atmosphere allowed time for contemplating the joys of Christmas and honoring Jesus for the healing He brought in their lives. The trees hung heavy with thick, white icing, and the wind danced about, daring it to remain, whistling its mysterious melody. A guardian invaded their winter haven and planted a single rose, bringing a splendor this couple would cherish. They would love and nurture this gift as their own. This present - this child - would be the greatest offering and the hardest sacrifice they had ever known.

They packed their belongings and made their way down the slippery path to the SUV. The overnight weather created some treacherous roadways, but Brian was confident he could get them safely down the mountain. He was much more preoccupied about the deception they would be creating to conceal the truth of the baby. Maria leaned against the door admiring Brian's strong jaw, tanned face and ocean blue eyes. She couldn't help but notice the tension creasing his forehead. Lovingly, she took hold of his solid bicep, then slid her arms about his waist.

"May we go in, sit down and share today's devotional please?" she said.

"Hon, we are running behind, and the meteorologists are predicting more snow."

She stood tall with an elongated neck, auburn hair playing gracefully around her face, and hand on her hips poised in her most sexy stance. He looked into her brilliant blue eyes and pleading expression. His will melted.

"Okay, not a lot of discussion though. I'm not up for much talking right now. No, trying to fix me this morning." He winked and grabbed her hand, leading her to the table where he pulled out a devotional.

"Let's read one of the verses, Lamentations 3:25-26," Maria uttered, sensitive to Brian's desire to leave. After reading the Scripture she continued, "It says here hope is a positive expectation that something good is going to happen to you because of God's great goodness. It isn't a wishy-washy definition of hope, but an action we must choose to take on purpose each day. Babe, will you pray before we go?"

He picked up Angel from the crib and held her close. Brian touched Maria's shoulder softly as he prayed.

The massive snow ploughs pushed layer upon layer of snow off the roads and onto the side. Brian stayed within the path as his dad taught him many years ago. He would never forget that particular day. They were traveling through the Austrian Alps. He couldn't have been more than sixteen years old. They took a family vacation to ski in the majestic scenery. His mom stayed at the hotel, pampering herself with a spa day. His dad pulled off at a safe patch and told him to drive. Terrified, he took the wheel. He learned at a young age not to argue with his father because he never won, and his dad was always trying to teach him something important.

White knuckles clutched to the steering wheel, he pulled the Jeep 4x4 onto the pavement. His dad instructed him to keep his eyes on the road, never look over the side, breathe and go slow, follow the path of the other cars or snow ploughs, and you'll be fine. His father's gentle, but authoritative words echoed in his ears. His dad's patience never ceased to amaze him, even when Brian drove dangerously close to the edge. He never yelled at him. After he felt his son mastered driving in the snow he congratulated Brian with a punch on the shoulder and a firm hug. His father always looked for opportunities to educate him how to be a better person and strong man. Brian hoped he could be such a father to Angel, inspiring her to be resilient and compassionate.

As Maria peered out the window looking at the ice cycles formed on the heavy limbs of the pines, she contemplated the words of Rojomen, "We are asking you to sacrifice your lives for this child; with joy comes great sacrifice. You can use your experience and the heartache of your lives for good and a greater purpose than you could ever imagine." The servant left nothing undone; a truck would be arriving tomorrow with the rest of the baby furniture while a contractor would add the addition to their home for the little princess. Everything moved fast like the tall pines whizzing by as they drove past.

"Let's go over what we are going to tell everyone." Brian articulated, breaking her lost thoughts.

"They know we've been dreaming of a baby girl and contemplating adoption. We'll tell them on our last trip we investigated adoption agencies and contacted one to begin the paperwork," Maria voiced.

"They're still going to wonder how we got her so suddenly!" Brian's panicked words filled the cab of the truck and Angel squealed.

Maria touched his arm to calm him. "I think she's hungry. Stop at the next break in the road, please. We'll feed her and talk some more."

Brian pulled the vehicle over to the next clear opening in the trees and Maria climbed in the back. He opened his door and stood in the cool mountain breeze, running his fingers through his thick wavy hair. He called over his shoulder, "I'm going to walk in the trees a bit." Then he pushed the door shut with the back of his foot.

"Okay honey," Maria replied, knowing full well he hadn't heard her.

She pulled Angel from the car seat, wrapping the blanket tight around her like a baby in a papoose. Angel looked into Maria's soft green eyes; it seemed as if the child could see through her soul. She sang to the baby as Angel sucked her bottle, playing with the nipple between her gums and tongue. After about twenty minutes she fell asleep. Maria changed her and laid her back in the infant carrier.

She lifted back the parka and admired the dark, soft crinkled rolls of skin on the baby's arms and the jet-black tight curls on her little head.

"Have you ever seen anything so gorgeous?" Maria asked as Brian stepped into the car.

"Yes, I'm looking at her," Brian smiled. "I'm sorry. Not used to hiding things, and this is enormous. Don't you think your parents will be able to read us? Won't they know it's all a façade? I'm not good at deception. I never have been. I remember when I was a child I'd pretend to be asleep when mom laid me down, but she knew I wasn't."

"Honey, breathe. It is going to be okay. We'll tell them the agency contacted us because the need was urgent due to the young mother's death. The family of the child is influential and accelerated the paperwork. They wished to have a closed adoption and nothing to do with the baby. They blamed the baby for the death of their daughter."

Brian carted Maria into his arms and looked deep into her eyes, playing with her luscious auburn hair between his fingers. "You are brilliant, but I don't know."

"Listen, this is as close to the truth as we are free to share. Remember, it's for all of our safety. Think about Rahab in the Bible. She lied to protect life, and we are doing the same thing. Remember who brought this child to us. It wasn't of our making. He will see us through. Trust Him."

"I guess you are right." Brian prayed, "Jesus, you know our desire is to honor you with our lives and to protect this child. Please give us Your wisdom and words to share with others, and help them to believe us. Amen. Okay, we need to get on the road. I don't think I've ever seen such enormous snowflakes."

Brian and Maria felt semi-comfortable using this story because it wasn't a complete lie. The child's mother was young, died during child birth, and the family was prominent in their country.

They arrived home in the evening. Brian combed the yard to make sure everything appeared as normal. He entered their home, secured Angel's papers in the safe, and checked every room before letting Maria unlock the truck to get the baby out.

He also gave Angel a thorough exam, including drawing blood that he would send to the lab. Everything appeared to be well and he thought she was the most beautiful baby girl he had ever laid eyes on. The likeness of the illustrated picture and dream he experienced was so near to the reality he held in his arms. He was overwhelmed by God's tender love and preparation of their hearts ahead of time to receive this child.

Maria peeked her head around the corner, "Honey, would it be okay if we give her the name Angel Nicole?" When he didn't respond to the question, she made her way to them, leaned over, and kissed the baby on her head. "What are you doing anyway?"

Brian stood in a daze, looking at the picture on the prayer room wall of Jesus playing with the children.

"Babe, did you hear me?"

"Yes. I can't believe how much she looks like the little girl in my dream. It's remarkable. Now why do you want to give her the middle name Nicole?" Brian asked as he sat down on the overstuffed chair and pulled her onto the other side of his lap.

"My best friend in middle school was named Nicole. She was a special girl and loved by all the kids. She never left anyone out. She battled cancer and fought an exceptional fight for three years. She and her family experienced tremendous trials. They were always kind to everyone, even during the most difficult of circumstances. One time after Nicole started chemotherapy treatments, she came to school with a bright pink beanie on her head. Her eyes shone like the morning sun, cheeks all rosy, and brought the class cupcakes to celebrate her birthday. She always thought about others before herself and was the most selfless person I knew. I would like to honor her and her family as they were very influential in my life. They took me to youth group weekly and loved me like their own child," Maria explained.

"That's beautiful, honey. I'm grateful you are my wife. You are compassionate, loving, and kind. He handed Angel to her. "Maybe when she gets older she'll want to be called Nikki; that is kind of cute." He smiled and winked at her.

"Maybe," she whispered, "but that will be her choice when she is older. For now, she is our little Angel." Maria laid her in the portable crib. Angel stirred for a moment and went back to sleep.

Chapter Two
EXCITEMENT BUILDING

The invitations were ready to be sent out and held an air of mystery that would stir anyone's curiosity. The mailing list included the family and friends they were the closest to. Dr. Ornsby and Dr. Ryan were invited because they were such an important part of Brian and Maria's healing process.

Technically the couple wasn't supposed to be home for a few more days, so they knew this would raise some suspicion, and they would have to be ready for any phone calls, texts or emails.

The party would be on Friday, January 1, giving them plenty of time to finish the addition, complete any last minute touches on the house, and pick up party items. But it would be no problem for the two of them to accomplish. They scheduled slots of time for each of them to sneak around town, achieving their individual event goals.

The workers arrived promptly on Monday morning to begin the construction process. Brian and Maria decided the little princess' room would be added to the back of the house, and they would keep the prayer room intact. Her room would be close to theirs with the small office in between. Security alarms and cameras would be installed in the house and around the property. He was willing to do whatever it took to protect his family.

Even though Rojomen, the baby's original guardian, was careful and secretive, Brian and Maria discussed the possibility that if he could find them, so could the princess' enemies. They would not live in constant fear, but they would take necessary and safe precautions. They would pray daily for a wise and understanding heart like Solomon in the Bible. Their hearts would choose to trust the God who brought them this child.

The construction workers finished on Wednesday evening. Brian and Maria worked frantically until the baby nursery was set up to their liking. Maria found a couple of extra touches to add to the entourage of furniture and fixings Rojomen delivered. The bed looked like a princess divan with a lacey soft pink canopy hanging above it and caressing the sides of the white plush comforter. Against the opposite wall the crib was decorated with a pink and white comforter, embroidered with miniature pastel roses woven amidst green branches. Brian moved one painting from the prayer room and hung it on the wall; it was the one with Jesus playing with the boys and girls.

"It's fitting; the portrait belongs here" Brian vocalized with pride.

"Are you sure you didn't arrange all of this somehow? Your parents had a lot of friends in high places that would do anything for you." Maria poked him in the rib cage.

Brian smiled big, "Only God could have pulled this off, my sweet love, and no human could have made it come together like it did."

"I know, but I can't help but wonder."

Baby Angel let out a piercing cry from the temporary crib they placed her in. Maria and Brian ran breathlessly into the other room.

He picked up the child and held her. "I think she has a tummy ache. All of this transition, poor thing. I will rub her stomach and do a few leg stretches. Would you heat up a bottle, please?"

"Yes," Maria nodded as she headed to the kitchen. She was a little disappointed Brian was comforting her; after all, she was her mother. But she shook the thought from her mind and reminded herself he was just as much her father.

The baby cried and cried; she would not take the bottle. This was the first time they weren't able to console her since Rojomen left her in their care.

Maria questioned, "Maybe she's missing him? Do you think she'll sense we aren't her parents? What if she doesn't except me as her mom? She's used to a man's care." Maria's eyes misted as she expressed her insecurities.

"Oh, sweetheart, this child will respond to love. Yours is deeper than anyone's I've ever known."

Maria smiled, "My mom always said I could love the dead to life."

Brian went to the closet and pulled out the vintage indigo blanket Rojomen covered her in that first night. "Maybe his smell will comfort her."

Maria swaddled the baby and pulled her close. She instantly relaxed in the comfort of her mother's arms as she snuggled her face next to the soft cloth and fell fast asleep.

After a long silence, Brian spoke first, "I know he told us to get rid of the things he brought, but I couldn't throw it all away. I knew the time would come when she would need to sense his presence."

"You are a wise man, my husband, but you do know why he told us to do it? To protect us," Maria compassionately rationalized.

"As soon as she gets accustomed to her new home, I'll get rid of it." He came close and looked into her eyes. "I promise to protect you and Angel with everything inside me. You know that, right?"

"Yes!" Maria resonated. "I think we should take some self-defense classes too."

"I was thinking the same thing. I'll be right back." He ran out of the room and brought his i-Pad back with him. "Look, here are some classes not far from the hospital. Maybe your parents can watch the baby on the nights we go. It could be our date night," Brian enthusiastically replied.

"Great idea, my arm is falling asleep. Should I put her in the basinet swing?"

"Sure, I will tuck the safety pillow behind her."

Brian designed a pillow that would allow a baby to sleep on their back or sides without fear of SIDS (Sudden Infant Death Syndrome). The support could be used with a baby lying on its stomach to reduce belly stress. It was still in the governmental testing stage, but approved by the Pediatrics Association. This item proved great success with babies having breathing difficulties or GERDS.

It was midnight Thursday evening by the time Maria and Brian collapsed on their bed. Angel was sleeping soundly in the nursery with the camera and sound monitor on. They tested it earlier that day when she was napping.

At 2 am, she shrilled, and Maria nudged Brian saying sleepily, "It's your turn."

"Oh no. I got up three times last night." Rolling over, he went right back to snoring.

Maria waited a few more moments to see if she would go back to sleep, but she didn't. Climbing out of bed and gliding into her lamb's wool slippers; she headed to the kitchen to heat up a bottle. They decided to keep her on the goat's milk since it was what she was accustomed too. A chill ran down her spine, "Brrrr, it's not supposed to be this cold in Arizona."

Angel was red-faced by the time her mama reached her and gently pulled her out of the crib. Maria sweetly sang a lullaby to the baby as she fed, burped and then rocked Angel in the Valencia angora glider. Her eyes hung heavy like the weight dumped on a body builder increasing his lifting capacity for the first time. She was about to fall asleep herself when Angel started wiggling in her arms. Then Maria got a whiff of a pungent odor, her eyes flew wide open. "Shoo, Baby Girl, you are potent. I would be squirming too. Let's change you." Laying her on the changing table, Maria held back the urge to vomit, the diaper being the worst she had ever smelled. She quickly went back to rocking her. "Come on, Sweetie, go to sleep for Mama."

An hour later Angel fell asleep. Maria happily climbed back under her own covers, but try as she might, she could not keep her eyes closed. Thoughts played triumphantly in the cortex of her brain like a miniature pinscher tempted with a treat. She looked over at her husband who was peacefully sawing a log. At first she resented the fact he was snoozing and she wasn't, but she reminded herself how much Brian loves her. She admired the man he was and thanked Jesus for bringing him into her life. She lightly kissed him on the head and slipped out of bed so as not to wake him.

Maria went to the kitchen and made herself a cup of chamomile tea, returning to sit in her small but plush living room recliner. Her hand brushed over grandmother's worn leather Bible. It beckoned her to read the songs of Psalms. She couldn't help but ponder all the events of the last couple years. A tear trickled down her face as she imagined holding Isaiah, which she never had the privilege to do. The agony of missing him diminished, but she knew it would never go away. Angel was a gift from heaven, but one day she would have to let go of her too. "You are my strength and help in time of need, Daddy God, and I know you will be right there with me through this journey - until the end." Maria raised her hands high in surrender and smoothly lowered one to place on her heart. "You are able, Lord, my God, to do abundantly above what I can ask or think, so You do the work in me to raise this baby and enable me to let her go when it is time. I trust You and thank You."

Chapter Three
THE UNVEILING

Today was the day, the unveiling of their beautiful princess, "Angel." Even though people would think they were referring to "Daddy's Little Princess" when they spoke; in reality they would never know the truth; the baby they held in their arms truly was royalty.

Brian ran out to pick up a few last minute items while Maria took care of the baby and prepared some party appetizers. They made signs directing guests from the front door to the nursery where they would begin their presentation of this treasured gift. Brian and Maria asked her parents to arrive a few minutes prior to everyone else.

Eula, Maria's mom, was always right on schedule, so they arrived promptly at 4:30 pm, which was perfect because Angel was napping, and the rest of the baby items were tucked away or in the nursery. Brian met them at the front door and asked them to come sit at the kitchen bar.

Brian and Maria stood beaming. Eula and Aaron looked intently at them. She spoke first, "Okay, you two, you are about to burst with excitement. What's going on?"

Maria asked, "Now Brian?"

Brian nodded his approval and left the room. They hadn't really planned this part out, but Maria trusted him implicitly.

He came back in the room holding sleeping Angel in her elegantly flowing white gown and placed her in Maria's mother's arms. Eula started to cry.

"Mom and Dad, meet your new granddaughter, sweet baby Angel Nicole," Maria bubbled.

Aaron's eyes brimmed with tears. He was utterly speechless. No one spoke a word for a few minutes as they admired the baby. Then Brian shared the story that Maria and he discussed. They despised hiding it from her parents, but it was too risky to tell them. For now, Eula and Aaron were satisfied and welcomed this beautiful child into their hearts.

Eula took Angel back to her room and rocked her as the other guests arrived. Each one gasped as they came into the nursery. The room was a good size, so there was sufficient space for most of the visitors. Brian turned the speakers on in the living room, so Maria and he could share their story to everyone at one time.

The minute she woke up Brian took her from Eula's arms. The baby looked into her daddy's face and smiled. "There's my little princess," he joyfully voiced as he took her around to show her off to everyone, especially Dr. Ornsby and Dr. Ryan. They both were deeply touched.

Maria announced for everyone to help themselves to the refreshments and appetizers, hot and cold drinks, and later, cake. Barbie was late getting to the party, and Maria met her outside. It had been difficult not to tell her. They always shared everything. However, it was for Angel and Barbie's good.

She embraced her friend and told her the story. They held each other and wept tears of joy until Barbie spoke, "Enough of that. I want to hold the baby."

They walked into the house together. Barbie strode toward Brian and reached out her arms for Angel. He started to hand the baby to Barbie, but Angel began crying.

"Maybe this is too much stimulation?" he questioned.

"Or maybe she's scared? I'll get her blanket from the closet," Maria replied.

Maria headed to the nursery with her friend close behind.

Barbie scanned the massive room. The delicate colors filling the nursery blended into a smorgasbord of delight. "Wow, this is gorgeous!" she exclaimed.

"Thanks, now where is it?" She dug around in the drawer after not finding it in the closet. "Ah ha, here it is," She responded.

"What's so special about that blanket? Why couldn't you use the one on the rocker?"

Maria ignored her question and headed to hand the cherished item to Brian. He swathed it tightly around the baby, holding her close.

Barbie persisted as they made their way to the kitchen to heat a bottle. "Are you going to answer my question?"

"He is very good with her, a really fabulous daddy," Maria continued. "The shawl has been with her since birth. We think there's a comfort attached to it. It makes her feel safe and relaxes her."

As they walked back to the living room Maria told Barbie Angel would not go to anyone else after her daddy took her. Only Eula had been able to hold the child thus far. She wouldn't even go to Maria until almost all the visitors departed.

After most of the guests left, her mommy tried to get her to smile by tickling her belly while changing her diaper. Angel got a really sour look on her face like she sucked on a lemon. Barbie laughed out loud. "Can I try to hold her again?"

Maria finished wrapping her up and handed her to Barbie who was sitting in the rocker.

Angel allowed it for a minute, but then she emphatically let them know she was done.

"Is she sleeping at night?" Eula asked when she joined the ladies in the nursery.

"No, she wakes up every two-three hours; sometimes she's hungry, and sometimes it's like she needs reassurance we are there or she's frightened. Usually we can sing her back to sleep," Maria replied.

"When you were little you loved to be sung to, even as a teenager you wanted us to sing in the car everywhere we went." Eula hugged Maria. "May I take her now?"

"Sure, may I help you clean up?" Barbie asked Maria.

"Yes, I never dreamed how hard it would be to put all this together by ourselves. I will gladly take the help."

Brian and Aaron were sitting on the deck outside having a cup of coffee.

"I can't believe I'm a grandpa. Can she call me Papa? That's the name I called my grandfather. He was such an important part of my life. I stayed with him over the summers on his farm, milking cows, feeding chickens, bailing hay and fishing. He loved to fish and taught me many valuable lessons about life. I will always cherish the relationship we shared. I hope to be as good a grandfather to my grandchildren. After we lost Isaiah my heart was broken. I never thought I would feel this way again. It's amazing how easy it is to love a child. They bring such joy to our lives. Thank you for this opportunity."

Brian put his arm on Aaron's shoulder and smiled, "Me neither, Dad, and yes, she may call you Papa." Brian spied the ladies cleaning up and voiced, "Maybe we should go in and help them; it's getting late, and I go back to work tomorrow."

"That's right, I forgot." Aaron stood up and hugged Brian for a moment. "I'm proud of you. I hope you never forget that."

"I won't. Thank you for always being there for us." Brian responded.

Eula brought Angel to Maria as they headed for the door. The little family waved their goodbyes from the porch.

They were settling down for the evening when they heard the rumbling of Larry's truck coming down the drive. It made Brian apprehensive. He had never been able to lie to him. His best friend could see right through his demeanor. Maria shrugged her shoulders and stomped off to lay Angel in her crib, frustrated by Larry's late arrival. She turned on the musical bears above it. The little lights danced around the crib to the beat of the music and enchanted the baby girl.

Larry was known for being late, but tonight he was exceptionally so. Brian met him outside, "Hey, you missed the party. Where have you been?"

"You know me. I don't like big crowds, and from the invite it seemed like there would be a lot of people here. Besides, I would rather you tell me what you're up too. You've been so busy lately; you haven't time for palling around."

"I know. Sorry about the distance. Listen, we have some pretty important news. I wanted you to be able to meet her, but Maria is putting her down for the night."

"Putting her down for the night? What did you get a dog?"

Brian punched his arm, "No man, a baby girl."

"You got to be kidding me. No pun intended. Congrats! Don't expect me to be changing any diapers though. I will tell you this; I've got some news too. I've been seeing someone myself. She goes to church and everything. A real keeper, I think."

"Man, that's awesome! Well, we'll get together next week for a few rounds of pool or to shoot guns, okay? I want to hear all about this new lady in your life. I'm sure she is pretty special to catch your attention. I have to be up early. Goodnight." Brian turned to walk up the stairs to the door.

"Wait. I know it's late, but can I peek inside and see the baby?"

"Maria is pretty upset you're this late." Brian paused," Oh, come on. Talk quiet in case she is already asleep, okay?"

"Sure."

Larry followed Brian into the house.

Barbie came in from tiding up the sitting room and shifted uneasily, "I'm going to go now. Is it okay if I drop by tomorrow? I'll bring you a chai from Bergie's?"

She contemplated telling Maria the thoughts tumbling around in her head, but didn't want to spoil the joy of the evening. The words wouldn't come, even though her heart was reeling with loneliness. She never struggled with being single and valued her independence, but seeing Maria and Brian now as a family brought forth the deeply buried desire to belong to someone.

It took Maria a minute to answer because she was distracted with Angel, "Of course, my friend; it's been a busy week, so we girls will be resting, but pray for Brian as he goes back to work."

Barbie kissed her friend's cheek and leaned over to kiss baby Angel's head. As she did, the baby reached up to touch her face. It was a priceless, magical moment that brought tears to Barbie's eyes. "This is one special baby girl you have here, and I am your Auntie," Barbie expressed as she softly stroked her head.

Barbie picked up her purse and nodded to Brian and Larry as they strode past her to the nursery. Maria was not at all pleased and didn't mind letting the guys know it. Her conspicuous body language revealed her heart.

"Come on, honey; this night is special," Brian noticed and responded.

"Yeah, I'm sorry for being late. Wow! She is gorgeous." Larry relayed his shock.

Maria couldn't help but smile at Larry's comment. "Yes, she is. Now if you don't mind, I need to get her to bed; it's late. Thank you for stopping in."

Brian showed Larry to the door and gave him a high five. He was thankful he came. It would have hurt Brian deeply if he hadn't showed up at all.

Maria let her silky pants suit slide to the floor. Brian couldn't take his eyes off her slim figure. She lay next to him and snuggled her head on Brian's chest. His strong, secure arms wrapped around her. The smell of his cologne permeated her nostrils bringing a sweet chill through her spine, making goose bumps stand up on her arms and legs.

"I love you to the moon and back, my dear," Brian spoke quietly.

"I love you too. Everything went well tonight. My parents seem genuinely taken with Angel, and I think our answers sufficed for now," Maria responded.

"Yes, everyone seemed pleased with our precious gift. Let's pray and get some sleep. I have a long shift tomorrow."

Brian began to breathe heavily almost as quickly as he rolled over. Maria's night's sleep was restless and disturbed often by little cries from the nursery monitor. Finally, she gave in and moved to the bed in Angel's room.

The agenda was to get up early to make Brian breakfast and see him off to work, but sleep deprivation robbed her of the privilege. She never even heard his alarm buzz off.

Angel hollered from her crib. Maria consoled her by walking with and cuddling her close. It was 11 am already, and she hadn't heard from Barbie. It was unusual she hadn't called. She always followed through with her word.

Maria dialed her number, but she did not answer.

This feeling of abandonment hadn't surfaced in years. Barbie thought she was past all of it, but the last few days the thoughts plagued her soul. When her mom died of cancer there were few people she could turn to. Even though it was not her mom's fault, she had experienced an overwhelming sense of desertion. She never knew her father. Her mom became pregnant with her as a young teenager. Her father never claimed her and pretty much denied her existence. Pastor Stroke counseled her through this time of transition after her mom's departure. She grew close to Jesus and the Stroke family. After what seemed to be a release of this emotional torment, Barbie spent less time with their family and more time with her best friend.

Now she sat glaring at the phone as it vibrated in her hand paralyzed by the fear raging inside of her. Would Maria abandon her like her mom and dad did now that she had her own family? Barbie could not make herself answer the phone even though she knew Maria probably needed her.

Chapter Four
THE SEARCH

The transition back to work was harder than Brian thought it would be. He missed being home with Maria and the baby. Work was extremely demanding, and he lost a little boy to cancer the first day back. Memories of Isaiah flooded his soul. The old files brought images to the forefront of his mind, making it hard to focus. The hospital garden provided a sanctuary to pull the violent torrent raging inside of him together and a release from the storm within. He was determined to find better ways to fight this destructive disease. More and more research was being done on the effects of nutrition in fighting chronic illness. His studies would be taking him out of the country sometime this year, and he hoped Maria would be okay with it. If not, he would find a way to take them along. "The Chief," as they called him, wanted Brian to go to Mexico and possibly New Zealand to further his investigations through conferences by top oncologists in the field.

Brian's work in Pediatrics took on even more meaning now that he had his own little girl at home. His heart ached for the children he could not save and for their families. He often thought about the other children in the picture that hung on baby Angel's wall and the dream. There had to be more to it. The vision Brian had after the loss of Isaiah included five children gleefully running with Jesus in a daisy occupied meadow.

After a few weeks of the dream playing around in his head Brian approached Maria as she folded a load of laundry in the living room floor, "Sweetie, come sit down with me a minute." Brian coaxed as he pulled her close to him.

"What?" Maria asked.

"I want to talk to you," He looked intently at his wife, "Do you ever think about the other children in my dream, in the picture?"

"No, not really. Brian, you know we can't think about adopting other children until Angel is grown or he comes for her, right?" she questioned with raised eyebrows.

"Rojomen, didn't say anything about that."

"Well, it is a given! Our focus needs to be on raising her."

Baby Angel let out a yip, distracting her mommy from the conversation.

"Do you want to feed her, Daddy?" Maria asked as she stood and danced her fingers across his arm. "I will put these clothes away and start dinner."

Brian didn't get the opportunity to feed her often because of his hectic schedule, so he jumped at the chance. Angel snuggled against his warm chest as she ate. He sang Jesus Loves Me and made up a couple choruses of his own. Then he gently put her on his shoulder to burp her. She spit up all over his pressed white shirt.

"Maria, Maria! Since when has she been spitting up like that?" Brian yelled as she came around the corner to the room.

"I thought I'd try the powdered goat formula. I guess it doesn't agree with her." Maria retaliated as she took the baby and cleaned her up.

"Why didn't you get the goat's milk from the market?" Brian asked, perturbed by her answer.

"The goats from Steve's market contracted the flu, and their milk wasn't any good," Maria countered.

"Did you look online and try to find another source?" Brian questioned as he stripped his shirt.

Maria admired his buff shoulders and chest. She smiled. Holding Angel in one arm she leaned up against him. "Come on honey. Don't be so serious. I'm beat. You know I've a hard time getting on the computer with everything I need to do around here."

"Okay, I'll help you find another source of milk. There has to be a provider somewhere."

The phone rang, and Brian went to the other room to take the call. "What's up?"

"I need to talk to you. It's urgent. Can you meet me at the pool hall?" Larry begged.

"I don't know. Maria is cleaning up the baby. We have an issue going on here. Let me see if I can slip away for an hour or so. Hold on." "Maria, would you mind if I leave for a bit? I promise not to be too late. Larry has an emergency he needs help with."

She glared at him, hands on hips, "You haven't been home long."

He gave her the dashing smile she could never resist.

"Oh, alright. You do what you need to, but tell him he owes me."

"Okay, Larry, I'll be there in fifteen minutes."

As they sat on the stools waiting for their turn to shoot, Larry explained the situation, "Adaline (my girlfriend) and I had a huge fight. She says I've got to grow up and get a life. It's not all about having fun and doing what I want."

"Look, you've had lots of girlfriends. You seem to care a lot about this one. Love brings out the best and worst in us. We get to choose which one we want to live in. Her heart allows her to see beyond your wall of protection; she sees who God created you to be." Brian counseled.

"You think she loves me? I don't know if I know what love is. I never experienced it growing up. It was always, 'If you do this, I love you.' Sometimes I feel that way with her."

"I've known you almost your whole life; you've convinced yourself you're happy. You put on a front for everyone like you're gliding through life without a care, but you've not known true happiness. My mom always told me, anything worth having is worth fighting for. Do you believe Adaline is worth your best effort? You know the only one who can teach you how to love is God. He is love. You can't give what you don't have. I can give you advice and share my own experiences, but He alone can heal your wounds and instruct you how to love."

"That is deep. I know. I think I love her. I don't want to be without her. She is smart, funny, wise but strong; she's the most caring person I've ever known. It's not like she hasn't been through anything. We've talked a lot. I've told her things about my past I've never told anyone, not even you. She knows the issues she needs to work on and wants to. I'm struggling with it, but I think I'm fine. I don't want to re-live the past. It's behind us."

"Friend, it sounds like you are at a fork in the road. You have some hard decisions to make. Maybe you should consider talking to Pastor Stroke. He cares about you and would help. Do you want to pray and invite Jesus to heal these areas of your life?"

Larry sat quietly, looking down at his hands, and inhaled deeply. "I don't know."

"Brother, there is no time like right now. Jesus died for you and loves you deeply. He wants you to experience a relationship like you've never known. I'd love to be able to lead you down that path. What do you say?"

"Okay, I'm as ready as I'm ever going to be."

Brian led him in a prayer.

Larry lifted his head high. "I feel lighter. Thank you."

"No problem." Brain hugged him.

Larry shifted his head to look at his friend. "You know I'm a private person. I don't like other people knowing my business. I'll think about talking to pastor."

"He likes to shoot pool too." Brian smiled

"It's our cue. Brother, I don't want to lose her." The two friends hugged.

They played a couple rounds of pool.

"I'll check on you next week," Brian assured as he patted his friend on the shoulder and headed for his car.

Brian sat at his computer at home. The search for goat's milk was on; the farmers in several states were having a problem with this new string of the flu affecting their animals. Milk and dairy products skyrocketed. Goat's milk was impossible to locate.

It was becoming quite the concern for Brian and Maria. Baby Angel was not tolerating the powdered goat's milk, or any other formula they had tried.

Brian came in from work one evening grinning from ear to ear. "I think I've found a solution. In fact, I don't know why I didn't think of it before." His face took on a serious expression with his forehead all crinkled above his eyes. "But it could be painful for you." He pulled his laptop from under his arm, laid it on the table and took Angel from her mother's arms.

"I'll be right back," he whispered. He kissed Angel on the head and laid her in the port-a-crib in the den. "I was doing some research; there is no reason why you couldn't breastfeed our baby. We could purchase the herbs to help you lactate. Getting her to latch on would be one of the most difficult parts and the sucking from her should help bring your milk in. I'm not saying it would be easy; it works for some babies and not for others. I bought this kit; it includes a formula pouch and tube to run down to your nipple so she will get milk, and it will encourage her to latch on and suck. I purchased the book and DVD to help you. They have a nurse practitioner who will even do home visits, if you need it. You always wanted to breastfeed, and this will give you the chance to fulfill a dream. It reminds me of the Scripture that says God will give you the desires of your heart, if you delight yourself in Him and you definitely bring pleasure to Him."

Maria sat with her mouth gaping open and eyes the size of saucers.

"Well, what do you think?" Brian asked.

"I'm not sure; I never knew anything like this was possible. I never dreamed of nursing another baby after losing Isaiah." She got up and walked over to look out the window.

The fluorescent moonlight cascaded over the brilliant color of her Double Delight roses and reflected the flooding emotions penetrating her soul. Tears trickled down Maria's face.

Brian arose and wrapped his arms around her. "Honey, I'm not pressuring you; we can find another way."

"I'm not saying I won't. It's a lot to take in. I'll look at the material tomorrow."

"Okay, honey; I'll support whatever you decide. Think about it. I'm going to go check on our girl."

As Brian rounded the corner he screamed at Maria, "Get my bag!" He jerked baby Angel up and held her upside down, applying forceful thrusts to her back. She had thrown up again, and it blocked her airway. Maria handed Brian the suction cup. "She's not breathing! Call 9-1-1!"

Brian suctioned Angel's nose, throat, and began chest compressions. She coughed and then began labored breathing on her own. Her little body was shaking and her skin bluish.

The ambulance drivers started her on oxygen right away.

Brian saw the terror in his wife's eyes. "Maria, it's going to be okay; jump in the ambulance. I will follow in the car." Brian encouraged, squeezing his wife's hands.

Brian told the emergency room doctor what happened and the difficulty of Angel keeping food down the last couple of weeks.

"Good thing you have lightning fast reflexes and are trained in CPR; you may have lost her otherwise. Her oxygen saturation is low, but she's responding well. Her color is returning; I'd like to run a few more tests with your permission?"

"Certainly," Brian acknowledged.

Maria held baby Angel's hand as she lay with an eerie stillness, IV running from her fragile arm and an oxygen mask on her small face.

"Brian, please tell me we won't lose her. This isn't supposed to be happening. I'll breastfeed her. She is our little girl, and I want her to know how much we love her," Maria broke down and sobbed.

He gently held her face in his hands. "Maria, we won't lose her. She had a bad reaction to the formula. Mucus was blocking her airway, and she is too little to project it out herself. We'll keep a close watch on her. I'm sure your breast milk will prevent this from happening again, but to make sure, I want her to sleep upright until we're sure she's okay."

The emergency room doctor came back a few hours later, "The tests all came back normal. There is no fluid in her lungs and her O2 saturations are almost back to normal. What formula did you give her today?"

"I tried the amino acid-based formula. The goat, synthetic and dairy formulas cause serious issues. She throws everything up; often it comes out projectile, and at times it's as if she stops breathing for a few seconds. It's alarming."

"She's definitely allergic to the amino base. I wouldn't recommend using it again. I'm going to give you the name of a specialist who might be able to assist. Follow up with him and we'll release her within the next few hours, if she continues to improve."

"Yes, we will. Thank you," Brian affirmed as he shook the doctor's hand.

The nurse came in a few hours later to remove the baby's IV and oxygen. Angel squealed. Maria scooped her up, held her close and assured, "Mommy's here, sweetheart, Mommy's here." She hummed the lullaby Rojomen sung the first night. The baby melted into her arms.

Brian signed the release papers and listened patiently to the nurse's instructions.

By the time they arrived home it was well past midnight. They were both exhausted, but neither could sleep.

"Thank God I'm off today," Brian said as he lay in his recliner with Angel on his chest.

"I'm grateful for that. I don't know what I would've done if you hadn't been home when this happened," Maria admitted.

"You would have done exactly what I did."

"I don't know; you were like Superman in your response, my hero." She winked at him as she lay sprawled on the couch under her comfy fleece blanket.

They talked until they drifted off to sleep. Brian's strong arms snuggled baby and they breathed simultaneously together.

A few hours later, the phone jolted Angel awake, and she screeched. Brian got up and silenced the phone before it woke Maria. Her face was still buried beneath the covers.

He took Angel into the kitchen and made a bottle with the goat's milk powder. He prayed silently, "Lord, please let this formula stay down; protect our baby, and keep her healthy."

He fed her two ounces at a time, giving long intervals in between, burping her after each serving, hoping this might help. She did fine until the sixth ounce, and then it all came up again, down his back, and onto the floor. By this time Maria was awake and moved in quickly to help clean up the mess.

"Maybe we should contact Rojomen," Maria voiced.

"No, we can't. He told us only if our lives were threatened or she was in serious danger," Brian responded.

"If she doesn't get nourishment, that's pretty serious."

"Let's try breastfeeding and see how she does first."

Brian handed Angel to Maria, went to the kitchen to get the equipment, formula and computer. He set everything up on the table by the rocker in the nursery.

"Okay, let's do this." Maria said.

"Right now?" said Brian.

"Yes!"

They watched the DVD together the first time. Then Brian filled the formula pouch and ran the tube down to her breast. She lightly pressed her nipple to Angel's open mouth but the baby wouldn't latch onto it. Maria became increasingly agitated. The more she tried, the more the baby resisted.

"Relax, breathe; it will take several attempts to get your baby to latch on," the video resounded again.

"Would you like me to turn this off and play your *Mother's Heart* CD?" Brian asked.

"Yes, that would be wonderful. Also, a cup of chamomile tea might help. Thanks honey."

"You got it."

Maria arose from the chair and set everything aside to change Angel. "There you have it, my little one; you needed a clean diaper. Now you will latch on for your mommy." She kissed her baby on the head and wrapped her tightly in a blanket.

She sat back in the rocker, placed the tube in position, took a deep breath and began again. Soon Brian came in with the music and tea.

"This is exasperating. I didn't think it would be this hard," Maria uttered.

"Hang in there; you are new at this. It's not easy, but it will be worth it. Maybe you should call your mom. Didn't she breastfeed you?" Brian asked.

"Yes. It's a little different. Don't you think? Won't they think we are crazy for trying this?"

"No, I don't think so. I'm certain she would be glad to help. From what I hear you weren't an easy baby."

"Okay now."

Brian took Angel and rocked her to sleep.

"Maybe you should breastfeed her," Maria jested.

Maria called Eula and explained the situation. Her parents didn't realize how serious the issue had developed into. Aaron had been sick so they stayed away for a few weeks. When they pulled in the driveway at dusk Maria's heart skipped a beat. She hadn't realized how much she missed them. She rushed outside to give them a hug. After their welcomed embrace Eula went straight for the nursery.

As Aaron's thin, pale frame stepped through the door into the light Maria's heart melted, "Dad, are you okay? You look horrible."

"Yeah, I can't seem to get my strength or appetite back. The flu nearly killed me. The doc says I'm all over it now and not contagious, but I wore my mask to be safe. Your mom wouldn't let me stay home. She pointed out that the fresh night air would do me good."

Maria never saw her dad so frail before, and she was beyond worried. "Dad, come have a seat over here in my comfy chair. I want to talk more about this later with Mom."

Aaron took a seat and grabbed the remote to watch the news.

Maria joined her mother in the nursery. Eula went over some breastfeeding techniques and showed her daughter the lamb's cream she brought along to help her with any cracking that might occur. The lactating supplements Brian purchased lay on the night table by the rocker.

"If you are tense, she'll feel it. Babies are very perceptive to stress. It's hard enough to nurse a newborn, but now that Angel is two months old it will be much more difficult. Do you know if the birth mother nursed her at all?" Eula asked as she reached to pick up one of the bottles to read it. "You can begin nursing prior to the taking these?"

"Yes, Angel's sucking is primary, but the supplements complement it and make the milk come in at a quicker rate. As far as we know her mother did not nurse. Mom, is Dad okay? He looks ill. You didn't tell me his demeanor was poor and his cheeks sunken in." Maria frowned.

"Yes, honey. He's having a hard time kicking this bug. He has a follow-up appointment and blood work next week."

"Is something else going on and you're not wanting to tell me?"

"No, not at all. I told you not to worry. Now relax. Do you want to try to feed her while I'm here so I can help?"

"She won't be hungry for another thirty to forty-five minutes," Maria growled.

"Why don't I make us some tea then?" Eula asked as she hugged her daughter.

Maria nodded and cradled the baby. She felt like her Mom was withholding information. She had a sick feeling deep in her gut, the kind you feel in a scary movie when there is a killer lurking in a dark place.

Maria followed her mom into the kitchen. As the tea kettle sounded its alarm, the outdoor monitor blared, sending a shrieking noise loud enough to stir the neighborhood.

"That's the distress signal in the backyard!" bellowed Brian as he grabbed his gun from its rack inside the garage and headed out the back door. "Lock the doors, and call 9-1-1 if I'm not back in five minutes."

"I'm going with you," Aaron insisted.

"No, Dad!" Maria shouted.

Angel let out a terrifying squeal, and Aaron took her tenderly from Maria's arms.

"It's okay, Princess. Papa has you," Aaron comforted her.

In three minutes Brian returned, "Another cat," he proclaimed in disgust.

"When did you have all the security installed? Isn't that a little extreme?" Aaron asked.

"My schedule at work often prevents me from being home in the evenings. I want to make sure my family is safe," Brian defended.

Eula brought out a tray of cookies, coffee and tea, "Let's sit down, eat, and let everyone's nerves calm down" she instructed.

Aaron bowed his head and prayed for peace, health and protection. He petitioned Heaven for his daughter to be able to nourish her baby.

Before Maria took a bite of her favorite chocolate macadamia cookie, Angel started to bawl. She winked at her Mom and snickered, "Now she's hungry."

Eula helped Maria for several hours, but Angel only latched on for two short intervals. Maria was about in tears.

"Sweetie, it took me two weeks to get you to latch on properly. You lost weight and scared me to death, but my grandma kept encouraging me that I could do it. She bore nine children; only six of them would nurse, but she was tenacious. She would tell me, "Never give up. You can do it! You can do anything you set your heart to."

"I know Mom, but it's difficult. I didn't give birth to her and maybe somehow she can sense that."

"Nonsense child, infants respond to love, and you have as much love in you for her as I have for you. Give it some time. You have more knowledge than I had when I started," Eula proclaimed, "and you were stubborn!"

Eula and Aaron gave their hugs and told them goodnight.

"Mom, call me with the doctor's report. Promise me," Maria requested.

"I will dear," Eula reassured as she closed the door.

Maria was ready to give up after fourteen days of excruciating effort. Her spirit and energy were depleted. While folding clothes, she listened to a sermon about Joseph. The teacher spoke on the peaks and valleys of his existence, how he trusted God with the events of his life.

Maria finally connected with Barbie and they agreed to meet at Bergie's.

She told Barbie as they sat having a chai, "If Joseph could persevere, so can I. In the end his rewards saved lives. For us there will be great benefit for our baby. It will bond us too."

"All I know is you look exhausted, my friend. Is she sleeping through the night yet?" Barbie asked.

"No, only an hour or two at a time. I think she's hungry. She isn't keeping enough down. I think it makes her belly hurt," Maria shared.

"When is your appointment with the specialists?"

"Brian hasn't made it yet. He wants us to give the breastfeeding a go first. He said if she isn't latching on better in a few days we'll call. I'm so sore; it hurts badly. Sometimes all I can do is rock and cry as I try to feed her. I think we are close though." Tears trickled down Maria's face. "I can't help but wonder if it would have been this hard with Isaiah."

"Oh, my dear friend, it could've been, but you can't go there. Comparing only brings more torment, and the, 'what if's,' will drive you crazy. It's simply not worth it. Do what you can. If it doesn't work, you aren't a failure. You got out of the boat." Barbie smiled and squeezed Maria's hand.

Maria chuckled, "I remember that sermon well. The guest speaker spoke on Peter and how at least he got out of the boat. The message was vivid, and I can visualize the scene even now. I can still see the rugged fishing boat, the gigantic waves and Jesus hand reaching out to Peter as he sank beneath them. The speaker made the story come alive. Thanks for reminding me."

"You're welcome; keep seeing the boat the guest speaker had on stage the day he preached the message. I'm glad your mom came over to watch Angel so we could have some girl time."

"Me too. I'm also worried about my Dad. He's been real sick. I feel like there's something terribly wrong. But my emotions are everywhere and I could be reading something into nothing."

"Look, you have enough on your plate. You can't take this on yourself. You've got to cast all that care on Jesus."

"Yeah, you're right. Will you pray for me?" Maria asked.

Barbie grabbed Maria's hands and prayed. They finished their drinks and headed to the mall for a little shopping.

Barbie wanted desperately to share the emotions she dealt with recently, but she stuffed them, not wanting to further burden her friend. Maria questioned her once, prodding to see if she was okay, but she played it off. She did share with Maria about her part-time job and her desire to go back to college.

Several hours later they returned home. Maria found her mom in the prayer room with a red nose and puffy eyes.

"Mom, are you okay?" Maria inquired. But before Eula could answer, Angel wailed from the other room.

"Let's try getting her to latch on good before I go." Eula suggested, patting her daughter's arm.

"Mom, you didn't answer my question. Are you okay?" Maria asked as she pulled Angel from the swing and sat in the rocker.

"Yes, honey."

"You look like you were crying when I came in. Your face is filled with anxiety." Maria was trying not to be too pushy.

"We'll talk later. I needed a good cry. I'm okay for now. I brought you a little something." Eula went out of the room and came back with a box. She took out a small DVD player and plugged it into the outlet. As she pushed play, Scripture accompanied the most exquisite nature scenes with sparkling waterfalls, crisp snow, a variety of colorful flowers, and fields of vivacious green danced across the screen. The birds methodically raised their voices to the heavens. The water and wind played a majestic symphony of music.

"Oh mom, it's full of God's splendor. Thank you!"

"Maybe it will help you relax. I want you to try feeding her without the tube, okay?"

Maria snuggled the baby close to her and rubbed a nipple across Angel's lips to stimulate feeding. At first Angel refused, but as Maria focused on the scenes before her she could feel her muscles relax. She breathed in, counted to ten and pressed the child's pursued pink lips against her skin. Slowly Angel opened her mouth and took the nipple, sucking hard. Maria winced in pain, but could feel moisture on her breast.

"She's got it!" Her mom was elated.

Maria queried, "Mom, is it possible? I believe my milk is in. I can feel it."

"It is probably the colostrum, which is good for her. Rub it on your nipples; it will help them heal. Your milk will drop before long. Angel will be satisfied, which will bring some relief to both of you" Eula instructed.

"She acts like she's starving."

"She is. Feed her fifteen to twenty minutes on each side, if you can handle it. Enjoy your time with your baby. This will pass all too quickly. I love you. We'll talk shortly. Don't worry." Eula let herself out.

Maria couldn't wait to tell Brian. She knew this was the starting point. From here on out there would be no bottle feeding until Angel latched on well, no taking turns in the middle of the night, and no girl times out, but she was content with it. Her mind was focused on the reward ahead, a healthy baby girl and bonding time with her little princess.

Angel nursed every hour or so that evening for at least ten minutes at a time. Maria waited anxiously for Brian to arrive home. He walked through the door after midnight.

After laying the baby to sleep, Maria hopped in the shower to let the warm water soothe her sore breasts, and then she fell asleep on the couch. She awoke when she heard his keys jingle in the door.

"Shhh," she hinted as she pointed to the crib.

Maria ran and hugged him tightly. She whispered, "Let's go to the kitchen."

He followed closely behind her.

"She did it! She's nursing. She hasn't spit up once!" Maria rattled off.

"Oh honey, that's wonderful. Thank you for persevering. Thank you, Jesus!" Brian twirled Maria around. "Tell me more."

"She's eating every hour. Will she take longer increments as she eats more?" She asked, half-smiling.

"Yes, as your milk fully comes in she will get satisfied more quickly. The time spans will get longer as she grows. No spitting up?"

"No, but she has been gassy, especially as she sucks." Maria smirked.

"That's normal. I'm pleased." He hugged Maria. "You deserve a jewel, a treat. What would you like? A memento to mark this special occasion?"

"How about a Peridot, the green stone for growth," she bubbled with a twinkle in her eye.

"You pick an item out of the Jared's catalog, and I will order it, okay?" Brian offered as he kissed her cheek.

A cry came from the nursery. "I will change and rock her a few minutes, okay?" Brian encouraged.

"Sure honey, thanks," Maria pulled the magazine from the table and thumbed through it. There was a ring with a small green stone and sparkling diamonds surrounding it, but there was also a floating glass charm necklace she liked better.

"Babe, how about this? Then as we pass milestones I will add stones to it," she gushed as she walked in the nursery. Her heart smiled as she gazed upon Brian sleeping with the baby snuggled in his arms.

Maria gently took Angel from him and laid her in the crib. She woke Brian up and guided him to their bed. She helped him undress. Tucking him in she whispered, "I love you to the moon and back, my dear."

Chapter Five
HURTING HEART

Brian sat at his desk looking over his notes, at the X-Ray reports and child 357's chart. "This isn't adding up," he pondered aloud.

"What isn't adding up?" Stephanie from room 357 taunted.

"Hmm. Excuse me, what are you doing out of your room?" he responded. The thirteen-year-old girl stood in the doorway.

"And how did you know where my office was?" Brian asked.

"Well, doc, I can read," she jeered as she pointed to his name on the door.

"Oh, I see, a smart one." He relaxed and smiled.

"You seem to care, and you're the first person who has in a long time. Can I talk to you, Doc?" the girl asked as she sat in a chair on the other side of his desk.

"Yes, of course. Do you want to walk in the courtyard?"

"No!" she pleaded and coiled up with her feet in the chair. "Someone might hear. Please, let's stay in here!"

Brian closed the door a little, but not completely.

"Go ahead," Brian urged.

"I'm thirteen. Can I leave home? Is there anywhere else I could go? I'm scared, but I can't stay there anymore," the girl confessed.

"Stephanie, why would you want to leave home?" Brian asked.

"My, my dad," she buried her head in her hands and wept.

Brian handed her a Kleenex unsure of where this conversation was going. "It's okay. Continue."

"My mom left my dad when I was five because he was drinking all the time and hitting her." She looked Brian in the face and then back down at her hands, ringing the tissue between her fingers. "But what she didn't know…" the phone sounded, cutting her off.

"Wait, please, I have to take this call," Brian answered. "Yes, detective Riggs. No, I don't have any more information. I will have to get back with you." Brian kept his eyes on the girl, but before he could hang up, she was out the door and on her way down the hall.

"Stephanie, please, come back," Brian ordered.

As she turned the corner her mom walked up and Stephanie froze.

"Hi, Dear, is everything okay?" her mom asked.

"Yes, mom, the doctor here was telling me I should be going home shortly, right Doc?"

"Actually, we have a few more tests to run first. I have another patient to see; we'll talk later. Thank you, Mrs. Thomas, for escorting her back to her room."

"Sure," the mom agreed. "Are you causing trouble again?" she asked the girl as she took her arm and guided her away.

Brian went back to his office and called Ted Riggs back. The detective had been a friend of Brian's father. "Ted, she was about to open up to me. I have no concrete evidence, but I feel something telling me there's abuse involved in this case. Give me a little more time. There is one thing on her blood work I need to check out and an ultrasound I'm going to order, but if those come back normal I won't have medical reasons to keep her and I'll have to release her."

"I understand Brian, but she is underage; all you need is suspicion. I'll dig into the parents', step-dad's and grandparents' records to see if I find anything. It's good to hear from you. Wish it was under better circumstances. Keep me informed," Ted answered.

"Thanks." Brian hung up and looked over the records in front of him. Stephanie's roommate was about to be released. He would pay a visit to the young lady later in the evening to finish their conversation.

There was a pediatric call to the emergency room. Brian was focused on the near drowning case the rest of the evening. It was a sad situation. Even though the child was breathing, he was on life support. There was no brain activity, and he might never recover. Brian moved him to ICU and spent the rest of the evening working with him. The grandparents were babysitting. Someone left the back door unlocked. The child slipped out and went to the pool. There was no fence, and he fell in.

Many children in Arizona die every year from drowning. Rules were in place; fire safety went to schools, made public broadcasts, and highly publicized pool safety. In recent years the incidents of drowning decreased, but even one was too many. Brian realized that lack of supervision kills children, not water, but he couldn't fathom how a person would deal with the guilt and grief over such a loss.

At 8 pm, he finally made his way to Stephanie's room. He was exhausted but felt compelled to finish their conversation.

She was listening to music with her head phones and didn't hear him come in. She jumped when she looked up, and angrily blurted, "You scared me!"

"I'm sorry. Is your mom gone for the evening?" Brian asked.

"Yes, she left to take care of my brothers and sister, so Fred could go to work," Stephanie quipped in the revolting teen tone.

"Would you like to finish our conversation?"

"I guess," she shrugged her shoulders as if not to care either way.

"You were talking about your dad?"

"Oh yeah," she looked at her hands. "My mom doesn't know that my real dad sexually abused me" she coldly blurted out.

"I'm sorry, Stephanie. No one has the right to hurt you. How long ago did it happen?"

"I was five when he disappeared from my life, but I remember. I love my dad. I followed him everywhere. Why would he...?" Tears welled up.

"I don't know. Alcohol abuse does horrible things to people. People who are abused often harm others. You don't want to tell your mom?"

"No! My mom has been through enough! Plus, I don't know if she would believe me anyway. She thinks I want attention and that I'm acting out because she married Fred."

"Where's your dad, Stephanie?"

"I don't know; we haven't heard from him in years. I don't want anything bad to happen to my dad. Please, Dr. Brian," she pleaded.

"Stephanie, I know you care about your dad, but we don't want him hurting any other children, now do we?"

She put her head in her hands, "No!"

"Code blue pediatric ICU, bed one. Code blue pediatric ICU, bed one!" rang out over the intercom.

"I have to go," Brian ran from the room to the pediatric ICU. He tried to resuscitate the drowning victim, but the boy was already on the other side; there was nothing he could do to save him.

Brian gave the news to the grief-stricken family and went to his office to sign the death certificate. He grieved and prayed. All he could see when he laid his head on his desk was a picture on his wall of a little boy waving on the other side of a river, fishing pole in his hand and a cap on his sandy blonde hair, grinning from ear to ear.

It was late, and he fell asleep on his desk. A light tapping on his door awoke him.

"Dr. Brian, are you still here?" a voice whispered into the night.

"Yes, Stephanie. Come in. What are you doing up this late?" Brian eyed the clock on his wall. It was 2 am. Maria must be worried sick, he thought.

"I can't sleep. I'm really cold. I keep having nightmares."

"Let me call my wife. Then we can talk." Brian dialed his home number, and Maria answered. "Honey, I'm still at the hospital. It's been a tough day. I can't talk right now. I'll explain everything when

I get home. I think I'll sleep a few hours in the staff lounge, do my rounds, and then come home around 8, okay?"

Maria was disappointed, but told him okay and to get home safe before hanging up.

"Do you have kids?" Stephanie asked with furrowed brow.

"Yes," Brian confirmed as he took the picture she picked up from his desk. "That is my son who passed away at birth, and this is my daughter," he declared, handing her another picture of baby Angel.

"My dad isn't the only one who hurt me. Several of Mom's boyfriends and…" her eyes trailed off following to her feet. She rocked back and forth in an uneasy motion.

"Stephanie, who else hurt you?" Brian felt his temper rising, but he started praying inwardly to calm himself and gain control.

"He said he loved me. I know it sounds crazy, but I wanted someone to love me. I've always felt fat, ugly and dirty." She folded her hands across her chest.

"It's okay, go on," Brian clicked the recorder inside his jacket on. It was too late to be in his office with this young girl, but he wanted her to finish. He was going to have to release her and wanted to get her help. He handed her a Kleenex, but stayed seated at his desk.

"I didn't want to hurt him, but last year I told him to stop. I wouldn't let him do it anymore. It was wrong. Then he had a stroke. Now he can't talk, and he can barely walk or use his arm. It's entirely my fault. When he looks at me, he cries. I'm humiliated and ashamed. My mom doesn't know. It would kill her. He's the only man she's ever trusted." She held her head in her hands, shoulders shaking and stood up, eyes wild. "If you tell anyone, I will deny it. My mom can never know, never. Do you understand! Her dad is her hero." Stephanie covered her mouth as she realized the magnitude of her confession.

"Your confidence is sealed. I'm going to call the nurse to escort you to your room and give you a sleeping pill, okay? I don't know why these things happen. I know there is good and evil in this world.

In time you can come to a place of healing and forgiveness. I struggled through this process when my parents and son died, but I can only talk to you about it if you ask. You have been deeply scarred, and it wasn't your fault. I'm sorry for your pain. No one has the right to wound you like that. Are you okay right now? Do you think you can get some rest?"

She nodded.

Brian called the nurses' station, gave them orders, and shortly after the nurse came to get Stephanie.

"Good night, Stephanie."

"Good night. Thank you for listening."

Brian went to the doctor's lounge, pulled a blanket from the cabinet, and laid on a cot. It was 4 am. His pager went off at 6 am, "Dr. Brian, we need you. Room 357 has a 103 temperature and is convulsing."

He administered a shot to stop the seizures and ordered more blood work. "I want an ultrasound of this girl's abdomen, uterus and ovaries stat! Give her more Tylenol to bring that fever down!"

"Yes, doctor. Her muscles are beginning to relax. Her temperature is 104."

"Give her an alcohol bath and then bathe her in ice. I want that temperature down now! Give her Toradol. This child has an infection, and we must find its source. Start her on IV antibiotics; do an IV push first, and get me a consult with Dr. Ornsby stat."

"Yes, Sir. Rebecca, get in here please. Take the restraints off. Let's wheel her to radiology," the head nurse ordered.

"Call me as soon as the results are in. Thank you," Brian handed her chart flagged red to the secretary.

He went to his computer and began investigating dormant strains of infections lining the uterine and cervix wall. He prayed for wisdom and asked God to show him how to help this girl. "Lord, she has been through so much," he pleaded on her behalf.

Brian called his relief doctor, "Sorry, Alisha. I've not been able to make my other rounds. It's been a difficult night. Please, start on the fourth floor with the O'Kelly boy. Thank you."

The nurse called Brian. "Doctor, the results are in."

"I'll be right there. I think I know the problem. Hopefully the results will confirm it," he divulged as he stared at his computer screen.

The ultrasound showed a tear between the uterus and vaginal wall. Brian used his light pen to trace the line of the infection. "There it is," Brian confirmed as he showed the head nurse. Stop the antibiotic and start her on a Vancomycin IV drip. Keep her sedated for the time being. I'll call her mother. Please, get Dr. Ornsby on the phone."

"Doctor, how does a tear like that occur?"

"I'm not sure at this point. I want Dr. Ornsby as a consult and have him examine her."

Alisha came around the corner, "Brian, you look horrible."

"Thanks." He turned to the CNA and requested, "I never ask this, but could you grab me a cup of coffee while I fill the doctor in?"

"Yes," she concurred, "I will bring it to your office."

Brian told Alisha as much as he could without breaking patient confidentiality.

"Please, call me as soon as she wakes up. I need to go home, but I want to know how she responds to the antibiotics, or if any further symptoms occur. Have Dr. Ornsby call me at home."

"Yes, I will. Now go see your precious wife and baby girl. You're back on Friday, right?"

"Yes, I need to call the patient's mom first, but then I definitely will."

The conversation didn't go well with Stephanie's mom. She felt the hospital did something to cause the infection. Brian knew she was scared and lashing out. The woman carried a lot on her plate, but she approved the specialist's consult. Brian was relieved for that.

Brian's heavy eyes kept him from seeing the menacing cat darting across the slippery pavement. The thud underneath his car added to the sullenness of the depressing day. He pulled over to the shoulder and rested his head on the steering wheel. Then he got out, retrieved an empty box from his trunk, and placed the lifeless creature inside. His mind told him to leave it there, but his heart chose otherwise. When he arrived home, Brian went to the shed to retrieve a shovel, and he dug a hole to bury the animal. He fell on his knees and wept.

Maria heard noise outside and turned on the porch light. She saw him hunched over on the wet ground. Monsoons arrived, and the weather was sporadic. The evening rain left the dirt moist.

She hollered out the back door, "Honey, what are you doing?"

Brian stood, "Burying a cat. I will be in, in a minute!"

He sauntered into the house and removed his dirty shoes.

Chapter Six
HIDDEN SECRETS

"Brian, I'm glad you're home. You look bushed. I was worried about you. What happened?" When he didn't respond right away Maria abruptly turned back to the dishes she was cleaning in the sink.

Brian was surprised. It wasn't like her. "I hit a cat on the way home. What's wrong, honey?" Noticing her hair pulled back in a tight bun; he caressed his arms around her waist and kissed the back of her neck. He tenderly pulled her around to face him.

Tear lines streaked her face. "I miss you, and I'm tired. I feel like I'm doing this all alone. You've been gone three full days. We need you too."

He held her and let her cry, even though he felt he would collapse any minute. She didn't understand the enormity of the problems he dealt with at work the last few days.

"Can we nap together for a few minutes?" Brian asked.

"No, Angel will be up soon, wanting to nurse. We should strap her to my chest. She's nursing on demand."

"I apologize, Honey. This isn't fair to you, but if I don't go to bed, I'm going to collapse."

He scarcely got the words out of his mouth, and Angel started to cry. He prayed, "Lord, tell me what to do."

Maria slapped the kitchen towel down on the counter and huffed off.

Brian climbed into their bed alone, and sleep came like a torrent.

Maria's breast burned with tenderness nursing Angel. She sang to her and prayed, "Lord, please forgive my poor attitude. I am grateful for our baby and Brian's job. I'm tired. Help me know how to find my joy. Give me the back to carry all of this and help me be honoring to my husband." A sudden peace came over her soul. Angel fell back to sleep with a full tummy.

Maria turned on the monitor, undressed, and snuggled up against her husband, "I love you to the moon and back. I'm sorry." She fell asleep holding him.

She awoke three hours later and jumped out of bed to check on their baby girl. Angel stared up at the bear module, her giggles echoing through the room.

"Your mommy's milk must be filling you up now. That's the most sleep I've had in weeks," Maria leaned against the crib, peering into her child's doe eyes.

Angel cooed at her. She picked her up and realized the ringers on the phone were left on. "We don't want these waking your daddy yet, now do we?" She turned them all off, including Brian's cell phone.

She sat Angel on her sea animal play matt and practiced rolling her over. The baby was getting stronger and trying to flip herself. She would grab the flaps on the hidden animals, but get blood-faced mad if she couldn't do it.

"Now, now little one, never give up. Keep trying. You can do it!" Maria coaxed.

Maria would place her back in position and put a toy in front of her to see if she would reach for it. They played these games several times a day.

"There you are. Thanks for cuddling with me," Brian gloated as he knelt on the ground beside the playmate.

"How is my little princess doing?" he asked.

Maria smiled as he leaned over and kissed her. "I'm a lot better after my nap. I'm sorry for earlier."

"Apology accepted. I'm sorry too. I've been distracted with work. It is intense. I wish I could share, but you're right, you both need me too. We are in the process of hiring another doctor. That will help." Brian commented, "I can't believe my phone hasn't gone off."

He picked up Angel and tossed her in the air a little; she snorted.

"Good thing she hasn't eaten for a few hours, or you would be wearing curdled milk."

He laughed and asked, "Is she going longer between feedings?" Brian scanned the room for his phone.

"This is the first time she has gone over three hours. I'm ecstatic. Every two hours was killing me. Are you looking for this?" Maria held up his mobile and then stuck it back in her pocket. "If you want it, come and get it." She giggled as he chased her holding Angel like a football.

"We are going to get you. It's not fair making me chase you holding her."

Maria squealed as he caught her arm and spun her down to the couch. He tickled her sides until she squealed that she was going to pee her pants.

"Okay, okay. Look, she's going to cry. You're scaring her."

"No, she's not. She's smiling, huh, Princess?" He used Angel's tiny hands, stroking Maria's belly.

"I give, I give, but I wish you would leave it off." Her smile became a disgruntled frown.

"Honey, it's imperative my work phone is left on in case there's an emergency. You know that. It is hospital policy."

"I understand, but it doesn't seem fair that we should have to share you all the time." Maria whined.

Brian kissed her head and handed Angel to her, "Let's go out tonight. You can pump. She's eating well now and a bottle will be okay. Call Barbie or your mom, please." He checked his phone, "This won't take long."

Maria heard him in the office talking in hushed tones. She didn't like this whole confidentiality thing. They use to talk about everything.

She buckled Angel in her swing, picked up his jacket and pants, and headed to the laundry room to start a load of clothes. As she emptied his pockets, a recorder fell to the ground and started to play. Her first instinct was to turn it off, but her curiosity got the better of her. Standing there with her mouth gaping open, intent on listening she couldn't believe the words revealed by the young voice. She stood speechless as tears cascaded down her face onto the ivory tile floor.

Angel started to fuss. Maria shut the recorder off, and laid it on the coffee table with Brian's wallet and keys.

Brian marched into the baby's nursery. The veins in his neck bulged, his jaw set, and with a firm tone he barked, "Maria, you can't turn my phone off! I missed an important call from a doctor needed on a patient consult."

"I'm sorry." Her eyes went to the baby feeding at her breast, "It won't happen again."

"Since I neglected to receive the call, I need to go to work. I'll be back in a couple of hours. I'm not on shift; I won't stay long. I need to check on a patient and make sure she's satisfactory. Call about a sitter, okay?" he sniped.

Maria laid Angel in her crib and followed him to the living room. "Brian is it the girl on the recorder? I dropped it and the thing turned on. It's heart wrenching to think a person would…" Her words trailed off into silence as Brian glared at her.

He took in a deep breath and exhaled, "We are not having this conversation."

"Did you call the police?"

"I'm working with a detective, but patient confidentiality is tricky business." He raised his hand to silence the conversation.

Maria flopped on the couch and sobbed. Brian groaned. He paced in the kitchen with words penetrating his mind. I Pet. 3:7, *"Treat her as you should so your prayers will not be hindered."*

He walked to where Maria sat and enfolded her in his arms. "This is a stressful season for all of us. Please, forgive me."

Her hunched posture refused to extend upward as her body convulsed with moans.

"Did you hear me?" Brian rejected the thought to let go of her and allowed her the freedom to release her emotions cradled in the strength of his arms.

After a few moments, she whispered a tender "Yes" and felt every muscle in his body relax. He prayed with her, and then holding hands they walked to the door.

Later Maria called her mom and Barbie, but no one answered their phones. That was weird. She knew her dad's doctor's appointment was scheduled for today, but had no idea why Barbie wasn't answering.

After a while she realized she wasn't going to hear from her potential babysitters. Maria got dressed and went to the store. "I will make tonight special anyway. Maybe daddy will be less upset with me," she told Angel as she tucked her in her car seat.

Brian walked into room 357. Stephanie's eyes were casting daggers.

"You promised you wouldn't tell! You promised! Get out! Get out!" she hollered as the remote came whirling through the air inches from his head.

"Stephanie, I didn't tell anyone. You spiked a high fever. I ran tests. Your uterus is damaged and infected. I had to call in a specialist. If we don't get it fixed you may never have children or you could die from the infection. Dr. Ornsby must have pieced it together. I'm sorry. We are trying to help you." Brian spoke with calmness.

"I don't believe you," she spewed. "My mom has been here all morning, begging me to tell her who did it. I refused. I denied it. Get out! Get out!" she yelled.

Brian walked out of the room and into his office. He paged the nurses' station, "Bring me the chart for 357 please."

He phoned Detective Riggs and his boss. He held a conference call and told them all he knew. Brian played the recorder unveiling Stephanie's confession. It was out of his hands now.

Driving from the hospital parking lot he felt despondent and wandered if this job was worth all of the sorrow and sacrifice it held. As he drove, the Holy Spirit reminded him how he saved this young girl's life and this incident alone made the heartache worth it.

Chapter Seven
GRATEFUL SOLITUDE

Brian smelled the tantalizing aroma of his favorite meal as he walked in the door, lasagna mixed with the scent of freshly baked chocolate chip cookies.

"I thought we were going out?"

Maria leaned over and kissed him. "You've bragged about how no restaurant in Arizona makes lasagna like I do. I wanted to spoil you a little. And I couldn't find a sitter."

"What I would love right now is your arms around me, you in your cute hot apple apron," he grinned.

She couldn't resist his tantalizing stance. She propelled her body into the air, thrusting her arms and legs around him, using her body to pull him into a tight squeeze, lavishing kisses on his face. Brian purposely stumbled backwards toward the couch and landed there.

"Wow. Now this is what I call pampering." He passionately returned her affection, rubbing his hands down her back. "How much longer to dinner?"

"It has another thirty minutes?"

"Want to shower with me?" Brian beamed.

"Sure, Angel should sleep awhile."

The alarm for the meal dinged promptly at 6:00 pm, but Brian and Maria did not hear it go off. Maria stepped into the kitchen and the smell of singed meat filled her nostrils.

"Oh, no!" she shouted.

Brian sprinted to her downcast body as she pulled the burnt dish from the oven.

"It's ruined," she groaned as she snatched the crisp cheese from the sides of the pan.

"No, it's not. Look we can just remove the top layer," Brian encouraged.

"Maybe you're right. We will let is set for a few minutes and see. Will you light the candles on the table for me and open the wine? By the way, how did it go today?"

"Honey, I want to leave work there tonight. I'm off duty, off call and home for two days, but thanks for your prayers today. I could feel them."

"Anytime," she countered as she chopped the fresh zucchini and squash for the salad. "These came from my garden. Aren't they vibrant?"

"Yes, like you, my buttercup."

After supper Maria buckled Angel into her stroller. They had a lovely evening walking in the park under the full moonlit sky. The baby continued to snooze as they ate milk and cookies in front of their favorite show, and gave each other foot rubs. Angel slept until midnight. She awoke famished and then wanted to play. Brian came in and sat beside them as Maria nursed her.

As her mother took Angel off one breast and transferred her to the other, Brian couldn't help but notice how red, swollen and cracked her nipples were.

"Is the lanolin not helping?"

"Not really. I don't know what else to do. I called the lactating consultant, and she is supposed to call me back."

"I'm sorry, Honey. Now that she is eating well, why don't you pump and use the bottle at times?"

"I tried, but it makes it worse. They are a little better," she smiled weakly.

Angel burped and Maria laid her on the play matt. She wasn't happy on her back and kicked herself over.

"That's funny. Good job, baby girl. You can do it." Brian applauded. She kept struggling to go from her back to her stomach.

"Wow, look at that pouty face; come here to your daddy. Why don't you go to bed, sweetie? I've got it from here."

"Are you sure? I would love to get a good night's sleep."

Brian shook his head, and off she went. He walked Angel around the house, talking to her along the way. He took her outside in the dry air and showed her the stars above. He quoted, "God made the sun, moon, stars, all the plants and animals, and God made man and woman and said, 'It is very good'! You see, my baby girl, pain and suffering were never a part of God's original plan. I know you are too little to understand, but one day you will. I love you as does your heavenly Father."

He rocked her in the swing and sang softly, "Jesus Loves Me," as she drifted off to sleep. She looked tiny on his chest.

Brian was grateful for the solitude. He prayed and thanked God for the blessing of his family, his home, and job. The moon shone similar to that of an eclipsed sun and encircled him like the lights on an actor center stage. The diamond dust dancing in the night sky reminded him Stephanie was one of the stars he helped save. She might be mad at him right now, but he believed one day in the near future they would talk again. When they did he would share with her the starfish story his grandfather shared with him as a boy. This story helped him through the exasperating trials of medical school. It is the story of a man who walked along the starfish-filled seashore, harvesting them up one by one and thrusting each back into the ocean. As the man reached down to pick up a single starfish, a bystander on a nearby balcony noticed this process and called out to the man, "What difference will it make? There are so many." The gentleman bent down, let the starfish slip into his fingers, lifted it high in the air, and remarked as he hurled it into the ocean, "It will make a difference to this one."

He would see many more tragedies, because the pediatric ward was a trauma unit and cancer treatment center. It was inevitable; the nature of the beast, but Brian knew God called him to this place to save as many as he could. Each time he lost one, he thought of his little boy in Heaven and pictured him welcoming each little star crossing over from death to life.

Brian let Maria sleep through the night and fed Angel a bottle at the next feeding from the supply she kept in the freezer. He fell asleep reading his Bible in his favorite chair.

Peeking her head around the corner, Maria saw Brian sleeping and snoring like a freight train. She snickered to herself, turned the baby monitor off, and went to make breakfast as quietly as she could.

The crisp crackling sound of bacon filled the kitchen. She made over-easy eggs in the center of toast the way Brian liked them. As she was finishing up baby Angel started to cry at the same time the phone rang and startled Brian awake.

"Sure smells good," Brian sniffed as he walked in the kitchen.

"Maybe she'll go back to sleep. Give her a minute; let the phone go to the answering machine." Maria encouraged.

"Listen, she stopped, maybe she needs a little lesson in patience," he jabbed at Maria's side.

Maria giggled. "Maybe you're right. She's a little young. Breakfast is ready."

Baby noise came rolling through the monitor, demanding their attention not a minute later. "I'll get her," she pushed Brian into a chair. Enjoy your food while it's hot."

Brian put the camera monitor on in order to watch them. "I love you to the moon and back. Why don't we drive to Flagstaff today? I will help you pack up for the day. We can go to Bearizona?" He said speaking into the microphone.

"I don't know; it's a lot of work for such a little time. I would love the drive though. I need to see if I can get a hold of Mom first. I haven't heard from them since Dad's appointment."

"Okay. Do you mind if I call and check on the young girl at the hospital?"

"No, we'll take turns making our calls."

"Or I can call your mom for you?"

"Sure, please do, after you eat."

Brian turned off the monitor, cleaned up the dishes and dialed Eula's phone, but there was no answer. He checked their home answering machine, but no messages.

"No answer, Honey. I left a message. Maybe we can swing by their house on the way back from Flagstaff."

"Great idea! They're probably busy. Mom would call if something was wrong."

She changed the baby while Brian packed the diaper bag, stroller and other necessities in the SUV.

They decided to take a leisurely drive to the ski lift, walk around the water and eat a nice meal instead of the bear park. Snowball's summits still danced with soft white clouds. It was a pristine day. The air was cool and crisp, smelled fresh, and the lake sparkled with remnants of ice and snow layered around it. They talked of future plans, shared jokes, laughed, and prayed. Angel liked the car ride and slept most of the time. As the orange and red glow of the dazzling sunset disappeared behind the mountain peaks, Brian and Maria headed towards home to see her parents. They drove in quiet solitude through the curvy mountain pass holding hands.

Beady eyes darted across the road, and Brian slammed on his brakes, missing the young doe caught in his headlights by a few feet. It darted into the woods. He pulled off on the side of the road to regain his composure and check on the baby. The lullaby from her musical hummed its enchanting tune. Her eyes fluttered open for a moment, but she remained quiet.

"Close call, my heart is beating out of my chest," Maria breathed a sigh of relief.

"That's why we pray. Thank you, Jesus, for protecting us and the deer. Let's continue our journey. Shall we?" Brian leaned over and kissed his sweet bride.

Approaching her parent's home, Maria saw the porch light on and her mom sitting in the dimness rocking back and forth.

Eula didn't want this day to come. She tried to rationalize the stalling, putting off the inevitable, and not wanting the words to play their deadly song from her resistant lips. As long as she didn't speak it; it didn't seem real. She would give it no power. How could she tell them? How could she lesson their pain?

Headlights hit her square in the eyes.

Maria jumped out of the car and rushed to meet her mother who hadn't moved up to that point.

"Are you going to bring me that sweet baby of mine?" Eula questioned as she stood and held the screen door open for her daughter to go in the house.

"Brian will get her. Mom, I've missed you. What's going on?" She looked into her mother's hazel eyes, and what she saw frightened her. "Mom, you've been crying," Maria pulled her mother into her arms.

Eula's shoulders vibrated, "I'm sorry, not like this," she sobbed.

"Mom, what is it? Where's Dad?"

Eula straightened up and wiped her eyes, "Let's go inside. He's in the living room, but prepare yourself. He's lost more weight."

Brian and Angel caught up to them. Maria took the diaper bag from his loaded hands. They walked into the house. He lifted Angel from the infant carrier, and Eula took her from Brian's arms. She held

her like a life-line you would throw to a sinking man. The warmth of
the baby's breath against her wet cheek soothed her frayed nerves.

Aaron sat in his recliner with an afghan tucked around him and
pulled up to his chin. His eyes carried dark hollow circles underneath
them; a skeleton frame looked pale and weak from the glowing light
above his head.

Eula carried Angel and laid her in his arms. She squirmed and
kicked, but he managed to kiss her on her head before requesting
someone to take her.

Maria and Brian each hugged him.

"Why don't you lay Angel in the crib. We need to talk." Maria
requested to her mom.

"If it's okay, I would like to hold her."

"Does anyone need a drink, coffee or tea?" Brian felt uneasy and
wanted to move about.

"Yes, thank you. Decaf tea for me with a touch of honey. Mom,
please, tell me what's happening. I can't wait any longer." Maria
demanded.

Brian called Maria as he headed into the kitchen. "Help me,
please."

She reluctantly joined him.

"Sweetie, give your mom a minute. It's obvious she's having a
difficult time with this."

"A minute?" She could feel her face getting hot. "Something is
terribly wrong." Hot tears streamed down her face.

Brian cloaked his arms around her and prayed for all of them. The
tea kettle hissed its annoying sound, and Maria pulled away.

They returned to the family room. Aaron turned off the T.V. He
looked at his loved ones with forlorn sadness, but then lifted his cup
and made a toast, "To Jesus being bigger than anything. There are
times in our lives when we don't understand, like when we lost Isaiah,

but we must choose to trust and go on with our lives. Eula, do you want to continue?"

"I don't, but I will," she seemed somehow strengthened by holding Angel. "This child is a gift, a precious jewel. I don't know how she came to us, but I'm glad she did. She brought healing to our wounded hearts." She caressed the baby and paused.

Aaron continued, "I've been diagnosed with stage four lung cancer, but I have to believe there is purpose in it. I'm not giving up until my last breath. I will fight, but I need all of you to stand in this battle with me. Can you do that?"

Maria got up and put her arms around her dad's neck. "No Daddy, no. It doesn't make sense. You haven't smoked a day in your life." She sobbed. "Yes, we'll fight with you, but you can't leave us."

She knelt by his knees. Brian joined her.

He looked at Maria with a sternness she hadn't seen since she was a teenager, "Listen here, young lady; I've no intention of leaving. I'm weak, but I'm not dead! Honey, can you tell them what we've decided?" Aaron's rheumy eyes pleaded.

"We are going to a hospital in Mexico, called Oasis of Hope. They treat the body to fight the cancer itself, instead of killing it with poisons. We are following a strict diet, juicing every day to put live enzymes into his body. The doctors there are trained in the states and use their knowledge to help fight cancer naturally. We leave next week. Can you look after the house and our mail? I know it's a lot to ask with the baby. We'll be gone at least thirty days," Eula concurred.

"Of course, I will come over and help you too," Maria responded.

"Dad, are you sure about this? The doctors here are trained to help you. They know what they're doing. I don't understand why you need to go to Mexico for treatment." Brian moaned with fists clenched.

"The doctors here have done all they can with my weakened condition and the progression of the cancer. There is nothing they can do but comfort care. I'm not ready to give up the fight and rollover."

"The doctors at Oasis have given us hope. They don't claim to cure cancer, but they have patients who have been given six months to a year to live in the states and they are living quality lives after treatment there," Eula added.

"May I speak to your doctor there?" Brian asked.

"After we arrive and have our initial consultation with Dr. Contreras you may. I know this is hard for all of us, but we must remain strong, nothing wavering," Aaron replied.

Eula stood and they gathered around Aaron to pray.

Afterwards, Aaron took Angel in his arms and bounced her on his knees. She cackled for the first time.

"Dad, watch," Maria laid a blanket on the floor and put Angel on her tummy. She rolled to her back; she got mad, kicked, wormed around and then flipped back to her stomach.

The room exploded with cheers and hoorays.

"Good job, Little Princess!" her Papa exclaimed.

Chapter Eight
STRENGTH OF CHARACTER

Eula and Aaron arrived at the San Diego Airport Friday morning as the sun appeared in the East. An Oasis of Hospital staff member was to meet them there. There were several individuals from business attire to casual clothing holding signs, some looked like they stepped off a cruise ship or were waiting to board a luxury line for the Bahamas, but none of them displayed their name. They gathered their luggage and waited. Aaron's strength improved little. He hired a cart assistant to handle their luggage. As he bent over to straighten one of the bags his head spun and he grasped for something to hold onto. Eula immediately moved to his side to steady him.

"Aaron, let me help you," she said as she grabbed his arm.

"Thanks, Hon," Aaron replied.

A gentleman in a pressed suit pushing a wheelchair approached them, "Mr. and Mrs. Banks, I'm sorry for being late. I'm José. Here, let me help you." He took Aaron's arm and maneuvered him to the chair.

"Thank you. Are you from the hospital?" Aaron asked.

"Si, yes sir. Oasis of Hope, at your service. We have about an hour drive ahead of us, and with the time it takes to get through the border, we must leave pronto. Is there anything you need before we go? Do you have your passports?" José asked politely.

"Yes, we do. If you can stop by the restrooms on our way out, I would appreciate it," Eula answered.

"Yes, Ma'am, I also have bottled waters in the van and fruit, if you are hungry."

Brian arrived at work and marched his way to the third floor nurses' station. "Hi, Sunday, did room 357 go home?" Brian asked.

"No, she is still running a fever, but she has been asking for you. Dr. Ornsby wants to do surgery and repair the tear after her white blood count comes down. There are signs the infection maybe decreasing," Sunday, the head nurse, replied.

Brian was both thrilled and apprehensive that Stephanie wanted to see him. He proceeded into her room with caution after a light knock on the door.

"Come in," Stephanie mumbled.

"Am I going to get hit with the T.V. or anything?" Brian jested.

"No, I promise," she commented.

Brian walked around the tray table to the side of her bed. With a concerned voice he asked how she was feeling.

"Not too good; I feel like I've been beaten up a little."

"It happens with infection. You'll feel a little worse before better. Are you having any other pain?"

"Yes, down here," She pointed to a spot between her lower abdomen and left groin area. "It burns real bad."

"That's expected. Did Dr. Ornsby explain why you are having the discomfort?"

"No, he tried, but I was pretty mean to him. I'm sorry. I'm so angry, and I know you're all trying to help. I found out my grandfather died last night from another stroke. Now I won't be able to tell him I forgive him when I'm ready too. He's gone now." She burst into tears.

"Oh, child, you carry way too much on your shoulders." He patted her arm gently.

Sniffling, she asked, "Dr. Brian, how do I get rid of all this anger? I want to believe Jesus loves me like I was taught in Sunday school.

I begged my mom to let me go to church when I was at Nana and Papa's, even when I was sick, but I feel lost and alone now."

"Stephanie, bad happens in every life. As long as there is good and evil on this earth it will remain so. God doesn't control people's will. If He did, we'd all be puppets. He gives us choices and at times people chose to wound others; hurt people hurt people. But you can choose to work through forgiveness and not let it destroy you. Do you understand?"

She nodded her head.

He continued, "What they did to you is not okay. It is horrible and wrong. Eventually you can forgive them for hurting you. It doesn't mean you will forget; it doesn't wipe away your memory, but it can ease the searing ache and bring healing to your hurting heart, so you won't carry all of this for the rest of your life."

"What if I can't forgive?"

"You can't in your own strength. The first step is a willingness to forgive the one who hurt you. You can say, 'Jesus, I'm willing to forgive, help me forgive them as you forgave me.' It will take time. You may have to say it a hundred times a day, but if you're willing it will happen."

"Okay, I'll think about it. I want to. I do," she urged.

"I need to examine you and start my other rounds. I'm sorry I can't fix the other circumstances in your life, but I promise to try to get you better. I will pray for you daily. Would you like to talk to a chaplain here at the hospital?"

"Maybe later, if it's someone you know. I trust you, Dr. Brian," she smiled sheepishly.

He called the nurse in and examined the girl. She squealed as he pushed on her abdomen.

He took her chart and increased her pain medication, Tylenol, and antibiotic. He told the nurse to call him if her discomfort or fever increased and to call Dr. Ornsby. He needed to talk to him.

Brian made his other rounds and was pleased the child with Lymphoma was doing quite well. The heart patient was being prepped for surgery, and the child in the emergency room was heading to ICU for a respiratory infection, but she was stable and her fever was coming down.

He made his way to the lunch room. In the corner he spotted Stephanie's mother arguing with a man. The burly bloke got up and stormed off. She buried her head in her hands. Brian prayed silently for her, but did not approach her. He nibbled the last few bites of his crisp ham Panini. The threadbare Mrs. Thomas marched headlong to his table and plopped into a chair adjacent from him.

"May I join you?" she requested.

"Yes, you may," Brian said.

"Please, forgive Fred; he is under a lot of stress. He lost his job today due to layoffs. He is trying to be a good husband and father to my children, but they won't give him a chance. They have been deeply hurt. It's not fair," her eyes flared with anger. "I deserve to be happy, don't I?"

Before Brian could respond an overhead page called him to the third floor.

"I'm sorry; I must go," he sympathetically voiced.

The charge nurse was waiting with chart in hand. "Her temp has increased, and her pain is escalating."

"Call Dr. Ornsby. I need to talk to him stat!"

As Brian walked in Stephanie's room she moaned, "Pray with me, Doc. Please pray for me."

Her mom walked in behind Brian. "Pray with you? What good will it do? How can you believe God still listens to you after all your grandfather did?" she lashed out vehemently.

"Mrs. Thomas, there is no time right now; your daughter is very sick. I need you to go to the nurse's station and sign papers for us to take her to surgery. We need to repair the damage to her uterus."

"Fine, do as she wishes!" She slammed the door as she walked out.

Brian grabbed Stephanie's hand, "Jesus, we ask you to touch, comfort and heal Stephanie's body. Help her be able to forgive, and protect her in surgery in Jesus' name."

"Surgery, I'm going to surgery?" she groaned.

He called her mother back into the room. "I want to explain this to both of you. I'm waiting for Dr. Ornsby to call me back, but I believe we'll be taking you for emergency surgery. We need to clean out the infection and repair the damage. There are risks, which Dr. Ornsby will explain, but if we don't open you up and try, we could lose you. I need your permission, Mrs. Thomas. Did you sign the papers?"

She handed the signed paper to Brian, moved closer and put her arms around her daughter. "I'm sorry, Honey."

"Dr. Ornsby is on line three, Doctor," a voice repeated over his pager.

"Thanks, I'll be right there."

Brian walked back to the nurses' station. "Prep her for O.R. stat! Dr. Ornsby will be here with his surgeon in two hours." He walked back into Stephanie's room. "Stephanie, the anesthesiologist will be in soon to talk to you and your mom. Everything is going to be okay. Dr. Ornsby will go over the details with your Mom when he arrives. They will give you medication; it will make you sleepy. Don't fight it. You are in good hands. The other doctor and his team are the best, and he will pray during your entire procedure.

"How long will it take?" Mrs. Thomas asked.

"I'm not sure. At least two hours. She will be sore when she wakes up, but there will be an IV pump. You can push the button if her pain level increases, and it will help her," Brian responded.

Brian went to his office and called Maria. "Hi sweetie, will you call our prayer team and ask them to pray for the young girl? Also, see if Pastor Stroke can come pray in the surgery waiting room. Stephanie's mom needs someone there to stand in the gap for her. Oh, tell him not to approach her unless she talks to him. Thanks."

Dr. Contreras met with Aaron and Eula, "I reviewed your medical charts and radiology reports. You do have multiple lesions in both lungs, and it is stage four. However, the good news is the cancer has not spread anywhere else, and no fluid is built up around your lungs. We would like to treat you with the Alivett method. You will have an I.V. once a day for twenty days, supplements called Immune Boosters, and we'll change your diet to include only live food, thereby nourishing the body. Cancer feeds on dead food; we'll take away its life source. Oasis of Hope doesn't promise to do what only God can do, cure. We have patients diagnosed with six to twelve months to live. Following our treatment plans they are living good quality lives, their cancers are not progressing, and some tumors even begin to shrink. We recommend going to our Spirit, Soul and Body classes. It will help you deal with the stresses and emotions in your life, which can also feed cancer cells, but the courses aren't a requirement. Your total treatment time will be thirty days and will begin tomorrow. My assistant, Cathy, will go over all of the details, costs, give you a tour of the hospital and cafeteria stamps you will use to purchase your meals. Your wife is welcome to eat with you; her meals are included, and she can attend all classes or therapy sessions and make use of the gym area. Do you have any questions?"

"No, not at this time," Aaron replied.

"What about his activity level?" Eula questioned.

"If he is tired or winded, he needs to stop and rest. Rest is key to his recovery."

He stood to shake their hands. "One more thing, my staff meets and prays for every patient each morning. Does this meet your approval? May I pray with you now?"

"Yes, please," Aaron responded.

Dr. Contreras prayed for wisdom and direction for Aaron's care, as well as healing and strength for them. His assistant, Cathy, showed them to her office and explained everything to them in great length. There were two options to choose from: stay at Oasis of Hope, which was recommended to benefit from all that the hospital provided or at the Inn across the border and be bused to the hospital every day.

Eula and Aaron asked if they could take a short walk and discuss the matter. She gave them passes for lunch. They walked to the cafeteria and talked.

Maria called; they brought her up to date on the information they received. She asked for prayer for the young lady in surgery. "Mom, I think it would be better if you stayed at the hospital. It would be easier on you and dad. I love you both. Dad sounds out of breath. Is he okay?"

"I'm okay, Honey; we walked a little. I'll get a wheelchair to go back to Cathy's office."

"Be safe. Thanks for the prayers. Angel is crying. I gotta go. I love you." Maria hung up the phone.

Eula called Cathy and told her they decided to stay at Oasis. She requested a wheelchair back to her office and for the rest of their tour.

Chapter Nine
MIRACLES HAPPEN

Dr. Ornsby walked down the long hall with tears streaming down his face. He knew he wasn't supposed to cry, but he couldn't stop the well of emotions. His mind questioned, "How could anyone do this to a child? I don't understand, Lord, but yet here You are in Your great mercy. The laceration was evident on the CT scan and ultrasound before the operation."

Brian met him at the end of the foyer. "What's the matter? What happened?" he urged.

He shook his head and put his hand on Brian's shoulder.

"No, no!"

A smile spread across Dr. Ornsby's face, "A miracle happened, a miracle. Follow me, Son."

They made their way to the waiting room.

"Mrs. Thomas," he announced.

Pastor Stroke sat in the corner and winked at Brian as if he knew something Brian didn't.

"Yes," she stood, "How's my daughter? I couldn't bear to lose her."

"We were able to clean out the infection. It was localized to her left lower abdomen and wasn't as severe as we anticipated. Also, there is no tear. Look at these films. Do you see the rip there? It's impossible for it to heal on its own. You don't hear the term 'miracle' much in the medical profession, but there is no other word for it. Two hours ago it was there, and now it's gone." He expounded with joy.

She sat down in a chair, shook her head and cried thankful tears.

Brian motioned Pastor Stroke over. "Anne this is my pastor friend, Mr. Stroke. It's been an emotional month for you, and he is here if you need to talk. Stephanie requested to see him if it's okay with you."

"Yes, give me a minute to process this," she responded. "And thank you, Doctor."

Maria picked Angel up and consoled her, "What's wrong, Sweetie?" She rocked her and bounced her. Maybe you need tummy time. She laid her on her exercise mat. The baby was putting her knees underneath her and trying to go forward, but kept pushing herself backwards. "Do you miss your Aunt Barbie? I sure do. Maybe we should call her." Before she could pick up the phone, it rang.

"Hello," Maria answered, but there was dead silence. A heavy breath sighed into the phone; shouting sounded off in the background. "Who is calling? May I help you?"

Gunfire blasted, and then there was silence. The receiver fell to the ground banging against the metal frame.

"Oh, my Lord!" Maria screeched. She wrote down the number on her caller ID and phoned the police. They sent a squad car over and took a report.

The officer explained, "We'll send this information out right away and get in touch with the local telephone carriers, but there aren't many pay phones. The area code should help. Remember, there is a possibility it could be a prank. Thank you for calling it in."

Maria was shaken and asked the officers to do a sweep around her house and neighborhood. They did. After they left she called Brian at work. His rounds were almost done, and he would be home within the hour. She called Barbie, but there was no answer, so she texted her: "Emergency. Can you come over now, please?"

Barbie called, "Yes, I'm at the store around the corner. I'll be right there."

Angel was cranky and wouldn't settle down. Maria washed her hands and checked her gums; they were slightly swollen. She pulled some ginger root from the refrigerator and rubbed it in the little one's mouth. Then she nursed her and put her down for a nap."

A knock at the door jolted her to the core. She peeked out the window and a man in a jet-black overcoat and hat stood there. Maria didn't know what to do; she eased away from the door, slid to the floor and crawled to the nursery. She called 9-1-1 and explained what happened earlier in the day.

About fifteen minutes later Maria heard Barbie pull in the drive. She collapsed in her friend's arms when she walked in the door. Sirens followed five minutes later. By then the man or what appeared to be a man was gone.

"Lord, this is more than I can take," Maria pleaded.

The police officer was kind and offered to patrol the area until Brian returned home.

She thanked them and accepted his offer.

"By the way, Ma'am, the phone has been traced to New Hampshire. An investigator will be contacting you."

Barbie stayed until Brian returned home. She reminded Maria, "I started a new job and went back to school. Remember, we talked about it the last time I saw you? It's been a challenge after being out so long. I found some of my mom's old English papers; her essays are fabulous. Thought I might take some of her ideas and expound on them. Who knows, maybe I'll publish a book in her honor someday."

"I think it's a great idea. I miss you. I guess our lives are going in different directions. Hope we always remain close," Maria murmured.

"We'll be best friends forever. I'm here for you," Barbie confided.

The ladies were so caught up in their conversation they nearly jumped out of their skins when the doorknob twisted. They hadn't heard Brian's car pull up in the driveway.

Maria flung herself into Brian's arms as he walked in the door. "I'm scared," she wailed.

He held up a flier that he pulled from the shrubs. "The wind must've blown this from the screen door. It looks like there is going to be a circus in town. I found this in the bushes. It should ease your fear concerning the man in the overcoat."

Barbie hugged them both and let herself out.

"This may have nothing to do with Angel; our number could've been dialed by accident in haste. Honey, it's going to be okay. Where's the baby?"

"In her bed. Brian, what if it wasn't an accident?" She started crying again.

"We don't know that. Let's pray, and I will call Ron to see if he can investigate. By the way, Jesus did a miracle today in our young friend at the hospital. I can't share the details, but God healed her." He took her shaking hands and prayed.

Days went by and Maria didn't hear a thing about the shooting victim. Brian came home from work and announced they were going to the mountains for a few days. She was overjoyed.

Maria shared with Brian as they drove up to Flagstaff, "I'm jumping at the sound of the baby crying. I'm like a rubber band stretched too far. I wish we knew what happened with the phone call."

"You're going to have to trust God with it. If not, you're going to stay scared out of your mind. By the way, are you ready to take those defense classes? I know your Mom and Dad can't watch Angel, but maybe Barbie can?"

"I am. I'll check with her. She's been going to school and working a lot lately, but I'll try."

Brian's phone rang. "Hi, Ron. It's good to hear from you. Really. Oh my. Yes, I will tell her. Thanks."

"What is it? It was a murder. I knew it! I heard the gun shots and screams. It was horrible," Maria snapped, exasperated, her heart beating like a hundred monkeys swinging from tree to tree using the veins in her chest.

"Wait, stop! No one was murdered. Someone was shot, but your quick response to the situation enabled the officers to rescue the victim before he bled to death. He was in a pay phone outside of New Bay, New Hampshire. You saved a person's life! Let's shout it out to Jesus! Woohoo! An investigator will be contacting you for questioning."

"Wow. I prayed whoever it was on the end of the receiver would be okay."

"It worked. They probably dialed us by mistake, and God used it for good."

The mountain peaks were glassed over with snow, and the cool night air sent a chill down Maria's spine as they exited the car.

Brian grabbed their bags as Maria unstrapped Angel from her car seat. "How did you find this place? It looks gorgeous." She said.

"Online, my love. Behind us is a magnificent lake with a surrounding walking trail and mature aspen trees. It's cold tonight, but the next few days will be in the sixties."

"It sounds perfect."

"Be careful, Honey, the drive is still a little slick. Try to walk on the thicker snow. Why don't you let me grab the baby? I will leave the bags and come back for them. Let me get you in the house. Here, give me your hand."

They creeped up the snow covered driveway. Brian handed Angel to Maria and used the code to get the key from the lock box. He struggled to get the key in the door and was getting more frustrated by the minute."

"Here, Honey, take her, and I will try." With a little patience Maria was able to jiggle the door open.

"Thanks. The good thing is there is a garage door opener inside; we won't have to do this again."

After checking the house front to back, Brian pulled the SUV in the garage and finished unloading.

"Why did we walk up the drive if you were going to put it in the garage?" Maria questioned.

Brian growled, "My mom went up a steep, icy road one time and the vehicle began slipping backwards down the mountain. I was young, but she screamed for me to get out and run to seek assistance. I fell several times and wailed all the way down to the bottom where I found two men who helped her, but I was terrified she was going to go off the side of the cliff. Nightmares ensued for weeks after the encounter. It's one thing to drive forward in ice and snow; it's a totally different scenario maneuvering backwards. I thought I had gotten over it, but I guess not."

They unloaded their belongings and put things away.

Maria handed Angel to Brian, "Daddy duty. I need a hot bath."

"I see." He pulled the baby carrier from their things and strapped her to his chest. The thought of finding the switch to the gas fireplace, slipping a relaxing CD into the player, and laying in the recliner sounded like a good idea.

However, Angel did not like being strapped in the *Ergobaby* and began screeching at the top of her lungs. Maria's cell phone rang, and Brian jumped up to answer it. This sent her into an even deeper high-pitched cry.

"Hello, I'm sorry I can't hear you. Shhhh. Shhhh. It's okay. I'm sorry my wife isn't available, and I can't take a message right now." He hung up the phone. "My goodness, Princess, what's the problem? You can't be hungry. We stopped on the way up to feed you. He tried singing to her, rocking her, laying her on the floor for tummy time, and making faces trying to get her to laugh, but nothing worked.

Brian gave up and stuck his head in the bathroom. Maria lay in the foamy bubble bath with her eyes closed and ear phones in. "No wonder she didn't hear you," he whispered. Putting Angel's feet in the warm water calmed her down. But he didn't realize the response he would get from it. When Angel's leg touched Maria's skin she jumped hard, her ear phone yanked out and went splashing into the water. She sat up and frowned at Brian.

"I'm sorry. She's been crying for thirty minutes. She only stopped when I put her feet in the water. Maybe she wants a bath?"

"Brian, really? She is teething and fussy. I take care of her every day; you can handle it. There is teething medicine in her bag or ginger root in the cooler, unless you unloaded it in the refrigerator already. Please!" she snapped.

"Fine, sorry for disturbing you," he retorted, walking out the door. His face started to burn, the red going all the way up his neck and ears, but he remembered how tired she must be from all the stress and how uptight she'd been.

Maria sighed, hurling her arms with disgust, "It's his turn. I need a break!" She threw her ear phones at the garbage, missing it by an inch.

Brian massaged the baby's gums with the medicine and pulled Angel's towel, rag and *Aveeno Bath Wash* from her diaper bag. "Daddy will give you a bath in the sink, my little one."

She liked it and kicked at the water. Afterwards, he gave her a bottle, and she fell asleep in his arms. He laid her on the pallet on the floor while putting her Porta Crib together.

Maria got out of the tub and shut the bedroom door not wanting to be bothered. She wept into her pillow and fell asleep. When Brian came to bed at midnight, he snuggled close to her, gently slipping his arm over her side, and prayed.

Chapter Ten
MOUNTAIN BLISS

Maria arose at the crack of dawn the next morning, knowing she needed time alone with the Lord after last night's self-pity trip. She gathered her things in quiet and made her way to the car. Spending time at the coffee shop would give her mind time to stop spinning and focus her in the Word. She fed Angel an hour before, and the baby was zonked out. Leaving early would allow her the solitude needed to refresh her soul. Daylight would soon arrive, bursting its way through the darkness allowing her to wrap the warm flannel around her and sit outside.

At the coffee shop the air was cold, but it was dancing with the freshness of a new day. She thought about the line from *Anne of Green Gables*, "Tomorrow is always fresh with no mistakes in it." As she basked in the radiance of the sun's illusive rays, dancing glowing sparkles of splendor played at her feet as it hit the railing of the metal chair. She pondered this saying and asked Jesus forgiveness for allowing herself to get caught up in the destructive force of feeling sorry for herself. She knew better. It was just easy to do without realizing it.

The sun peeked through the curtains and pierced Brian's eyes. He lazily rolled over to wrap his arms around his lovely bride, but she wasn't there.

She left him a note on the table – going to the store for breakfast items. Be back soon. Sorry for being grumpy. SHMILY with a purple heart drawn on it. He reminisced about the elderly couple who taught them the meaning of the metaphor. They used this saying with each other for sixty years. SHMILY means "See How Much I Love You." On one particular occasion the man went to war. His wife put a note in every stitch of his clothing with this pronouncement of her love.

Brian looked over at the crib where Angel slept. He pulled out his Bible and sat down to read. The baby started to stir, and he prayed. Fifteen minutes with you Lord, please. It worked, and she didn't wake up until Maria opened the garage door.

He opened the door and grabbed several bags. "This is enough for an army. I'm surprised you went down and back up the drive by yourself." Brian sniffed a bag, "I smell bacon, garlic potatoes, and cinnamon rolls. Yum! Yum! I'm sorry about last night. It was inconsiderate of me to interrupt your quiet time."

"Apology accepted. I'm sorry too. My dad taught me well. We took many vacations sledding in the mountains. I couldn't decide what to get. I figured it would keep, and we wouldn't have to cook."

"Okay, thanks. Can I ask you a question?" He didn't wait for a reply and continued on. "Do you need to talk to Pastor Stroke or Dr. Ryan? You have been under a lot of pressure with breastfeeding, your dad being sick, and the call. The strange visit didn't help either."

Maria scowled at him, "And how am I supposed to do that when we can't talk to anyone about what's really going on?"

"You're right. I'm sorry things have been difficult, and I've not been around enough. I know you're scared. You could talk to one of them, being sensitive to leave out any unnecessary details." He encased his arms sweetly around her waist and pulled her close.

She melted into his arms, "I never knew it would be this hard, not being able to talk about it: our fear, hopes, and dreams for her future. I'm worried about dad. He sounded horrible. Do you think this treatment will work? Angel has been cranky. Barbie hasn't been around in weeks, except for the night of the shooting. I don't know what's going on with her. I know she's busy, but it's weird when she doesn't answer my calls. The terrifying phone call was the last straw in this collage of stress."

"Maybe I can take a personal leave, and you can go see your dad for a few days?"

"Maria looked up at him, her eyes lighting up for a second, and then she groaned. "My milk will dry up, and I don't think I can pump that much. Plus, I don't know if I could leave her. This fear is strangling me."

"Let's pray, Honey. Dear Heavenly Father, You know all things. Minister your healing and peace to our hearts, and show us the way."

They sat on the back patio swing while they ate their meal. They fed Angel and took her for a walk around the pristine lake. The sidewalks glistened with snow and patches of ice. During the day more melted, but the freezing temperatures in the evening kept the lake and paths partially frozen.

Brian and Maria laughed as the ducks waddled across the solid masses of water. The wood ducks with their small frames and brown heads dove underneath the icy crusted ripples to find their meals beneath the dark depths. Shimmering diamonds sparkled in the pond as ice islands broke away from their source and formed crystal-like shapes in currents of the ducks' paths.

A bald eagle perched majestically in the top of the barren Aspen; his white head standing out in contrast against the tall fragrant pines surrounding it. They sat on a bench admiring the scene, looking at the grand mountain in front of them.

"I feel like God is always here, like He makes His home in these high peaks. I know the Bible doesn't say it, but it does say He talked to people often in the mountains, like Moses." Brian expressed his awe over such beauty.

"Yes, you do seem to sense His presence more. Maybe we could move here someday. I mean, after Dad gets better. We both love the higher elevations and nature. It would be a good place to raise our family."

"I would love to live here." Brian squeezed her hand. "For now maybe we should head back. The wind is picking up, and look at the dark cloud moving this way from the north."

Maria's cell phone rang, "Hello, yes this is her. I do know him. He is my husband's uncle. I would be glad to talk to you, but I'm out of town. Is he okay? I see. Friday of next week should be fine," Maria's eyes misted. "The man who was shot and called from the pay phone in New Hampshire is your uncle Ron. He is in stable condition. The investigator wants to talk to me."

Brian's mouth was gaping open. "Then he wasn't drunk?"

"He didn't say, but they are trying to confirm his story."

"I'm flabbergasted, as my Dad use to say. God works in mysterious ways. Did he say what hospital he is in?"

"No, my heart aches for him. I'm glad he is okay. I guess we'll find out more next week. Let's pray for him."

Brian bowed his head and prayed.

Brian and Maria were quiet for a distance, and then chatted light-heartedly back to the spacious, inviting and well-lit home. They talked of plans for the future, where they would like to live in Flagstaff or the surrounding areas, job possibilities and opportunities for Maria as Angel got a little older.

As they ate a leisurely dinner, Maria brought up a conversation. "Sometimes it feels like she will be attached to me forever, but it's not long and I'm trying to enjoy it. I do like the bonding time with her, and it's getting easier as far as the soreness goes. I long for more time to refocus and rest. I think we should arrange for a vision retreat when Angel gets off the breast."

"Yes, and you need to tell me what you need. I'm not good at reading your mind. Tell me your desires. Give me a plan, and I can do it, okay?" He winked at her. "What is a vision retreat anyway? Sounds like it would be fun. I would love to have you all to myself."

Maria scooted over to him and placed her arm around his neck; she looked into his irresistible eyes and kissed him deeply. "A vision retreat is where we take time away as a couple and makes plans or make a vision for our family, us individually, and even for Angel. We set goals in each area of our lives for the year. I've been watching Jimmy Evan's, *Marriage on the Rock* DVD's. They are inspiring, funny, and encouraging."

"How did you have time for that?' Brian teased.

"While I'm feeding Angel; it's perfect because I have time to reflect. The videos keep me focused. Actually, time to nurse her now."

"I can't wait to plan that retreat! Yippee kiyay!" He started laughing and slapped her on the butt as she got up. "I'll clean up the kitchen."

"Thanks. I think I'll pump extra, nothing is impossible, maybe the trip to see my dad will work out. Pondering those two journeys makes me feel better, especially contemplating the time alone with you."

"Do you want to watch a comedy or a romance tonight? I brought your favorite!" he cheerfully exclaimed.

Angel was throwing a fit.

"You know it! *Sleepless in Seattle* it is."

After feeding the baby, talking, tickling and playing with her until she was worn out, Maria changed her into pajamas. Her body was starting to get longer and her little chubby cheeks looked like a chipmunk with a full pouch of nuts tucked away in his mouth for the winter. She admired the baby's sugar and spice personality and her soft, shiny dark skin.

The next morning as Brian walked around the unspoiled lake, the sun glimmered off the water reflecting its brilliant rays like a mirror reproducing one's image inside of it. The magnitude of its immense power was only subdued by the quiet forest around him. A magnificent bald eagle sat high upon its perch; the bird's bleached head standing out in contrast against the greenery surrounding him. As he walked it swooped down, circling and made several passes over him as if to say, "Hi, thank you for coming to see me today." It was glorious and further reminded him of the splendor and majesty of His Awesome Creator. He breathed in deep and counted to fifteen, exhaling slowly. The mountain air smelled fresh like an unexpected spring shower.

Brian felt a renewed sense of purpose as he walked back to the house in the brisk morning air. This would be the perfect place to raise Angel. His contract with the hospital would be up in the spring of next year. They had plenty of time to investigate their options for re-locating.

As he turned the key in the lock he heard Angel cooing and Maria coaxing her, "Come on. You can do it; get those little legs under you."

Angel squirmed, kicked and flipped herself over. Maria applauded with joy, "Good job honey!"

"Hey, Babe. Want to go for a coffee?" Brian asked.

"Sounds good to me. Will you do a few more floor plays with her while I get ready? Maybe we can go by the visitor's station too."

"Sure, and I want to treat you to a spa day."

"Oh yeah. Now that's what I'm talking about. Thanks." She jumped up and threw her arms around his neck, lavishing him with kisses.

"Okay, princess, let's get to work." Brian tickled her belly, and Angel squealed. He sung, "One, two, three, exercise with me."

She did a few more flips before she was tuckered out. Brian picked her up and changed her diaper. He retrieved Angel's pink bag, made sure everything they needed was there, and loaded the car. The stroller was already tucked away in the car from the night before.

"Hon, you about ready? We are!" he yelled into the bedroom.

A few minutes later they loaded into the car and began the trek to town. The vehicle started violently shaking driving down the freeway. "We have a flat." Brian sped up and then pulled over.

"Don't worry honey. I will fix it in a jiff." He jumped out of the car, grabbed the jack and the spare. He let out an exasperated breath, "Oh, man! It's one of those little temporary tires. I thought they put a regular spare tire in here."

Maria rolled down her window. "Breathe, Honey. It will be okay." She prayed and opened her door.

"I can't get the lug nuts off." He hated doing any kind of work on their cars; it wasn't his gifting. He tried, but every time he did, something would go wrong. Maria felt sorry for him. He was getting more flustered by the minute.

"We have roadside assistance. Would you like me to call them?"

"No! I can do this!"

Angel started to cry. Maria stepped out her door and into the back seat, brushing Brian's hair as she went by. She started to unbuckle and pull her out of the infant carrier when he called to her.

"Maria, can you come here a minute?"

Maria consoled Angel, "Now, now honey, it's okay, Mommy will be right back," and she handed her a bright plastic pull and squeeze toy.

"Please, pray. I've one more to get off, and its being stubborn."

Maria thought, and so are you, but she kept it to herself, "Yes, I will. Heavenly Father, loosen this lug nut, give Brian peace, and help us call for help if we need too. Amen."

"Alright, ten more minutes. If I don't get it, then you can call."

She clambered back in as a truck whizzed by close enough she was sure it was going to hit them.

"Brian, Please," she yelled out the window.

"Okay!" He threw the wrench down, got in the car, and slammed the door.

He dialed the number to roadside assistance. Neither of them spoke for a few minutes. She took a couple deep breathes and opened her mouth to speak, but Brian motioned for her not too by putting his hand up.

She was hurt and turned to look out the window as tears ran down her face. Angel cried herself to sleep, because Brian didn't want her unbuckled close to the road. "It was too dangerous," he demanded.

It took the roadside assistance less than forty-five minutes to get there and change the tire.

"This whole day is ruined," Brian stressed.

"Look at me; it's only wasted if we allow it to be. We need to go back to the house, change and feed the baby. Then we can continue our outing. We choose if we are going to let it be the end of the day. Our attitude is everything. I don't want to let it disrupt the joy of what Jesus has planned for us today. A character moment was built." She wiped her face and brightly smiled, patting his hand and trying to lighten the mood. "We are safe, and isn't that what matters most?"

Brian's eyes misted, "I wanted to make this day special for you and pamper you like you deserve to be."

"I know, but there will be other days if we don't make it today, maybe a day I need it even more." Tightly squeezing his hand, she leaned over to kiss him. "I thank God every day for you, my sexy hero and friend."

"I guess you're right. I'm sorry for being such a jerk."

They decided to go into town for lunch and coffee at Macy's European Coffee House on Beaver Street. The staff fell in love with the baby and doted on her for an hour.

"Hmmm, they have a mushroom veggie burger, Maria. It looks delicious. Would you like it with a side salad?" Brian asked.

"Yes, sounds good and a chai too, please. Oh, don't forget the almond milk."

"How old is she?" A young, slender, dark-eyed lady asked.

"A little over four months," Angel replied.

"She is beautiful!" The girl exclaimed. "My name is Alesha. May I hold her?"

Maria looked at Brian, but his back was turned to her as he waited in the ordering line. She was perplexed as what to do.

"I'm sorry. I don't mean to be presumptuous. I lost my baby girl a few months ago." Alesha commented.

Maria smiled with compassion, "If you will sit here by me, you can hold her for a minute. She may cry. She isn't used to strangers."

But as the girl lifted her from her carrier, Angel smiled. Alesha's gentle expression intrigued Angel as she held her close, talking to her in baby talk. Her little hand reached up to touch the girl's face.

A teardrop formed in the girl's eye and slowly made its way down her Cherokee cheeks. "I'm sorry for your heartache. I too lost a little boy at birth. It is very difficult, but there is healing, although you never get over the loss. It doesn't have to destroy you. I will never bear children, but look at this sweet jewel Jesus blessed us with. Even in this blessing there is a sting; one day we may have to let her go too. Life is full of loss and heartache, but there is much gain and joy also. The most important thing is what we do with the trials and what we become through them." Maria reasoned as she placed her hand on Alesha's arm.

"I don't know the Jesus you talk of, but oh, how I wish something could ease this intense agony. I have no one here. My parents didn't even know I was pregnant. The boy, I met him on the train, and I don't even know how to reach him. Loneliness enveloped me, and he was there." She responded bitterly.

Brian was standing off to the right as to not disturb their conversation. Maria explained to Alesha how Jesus came to this earth and sacrificed His life for her, what sin is, and why we need forgiveness. She explained why Jesus' sacrifice was necessary and how very much He loved her.

She asked if she could call Brian over to pray with them. Alesha nodded her head yes. They led her in a prayer of healing and forgiveness.

"I have a gift for you," Brian told her. He went to their car and pulled his message Bible out along with a basic beginner's study. Maria's dad gave them extra copies of mentoring material to keep in their car when leading people to Jesus.

Maria was hugging her with Angel on her hip when he returned.

"I've never heard God spoken of in this way before. Thank you for sharing your story."

"Here's my number. You call me if you need to talk. Let's look on the internet and see if we can find a church for you. We could take you tomorrow, if you like?" Maria promised.

"Okay," the girl sounded apprehensive.

"I'm sorry. I don't mean to push you. It's important to get plugged in somewhere you

can learn and grow."

"I appreciate what you've done, but…" she hesitated, "I will be alright." Alesha gave

Maria a hug. "Thank you." She lightly touched the baby's cheek and walked out of the coffee shop.

Maria started to follow her, but Brian put his hand gently on her shoulder. "Honey, she

has our number. She'll call when she is ready."

Angel started to whine.

"She's hungry; I'll go to the car and feed her." Maria's voice quivered with disappointment.

Despite the rough start to the day, they scarfed up a mouthwatering meal and spent a delightful evening together.

Later that evening they sat in the dimly lit Asian restaurant observing the puffer fish swimming in the tank, Brian said, "Isn't it amazing how God orchestrated this whole afternoon? If the flat tire didn't occur, we wouldn't have gone to the coffee shop at the exact time we did."

"And we wouldn't have met Alesha. We planted a seed and watered it." Maria exchanged.

"The Scriptures say God works all things out for good. We sure saw that verse displayed in front of us today."

Brian and Maria toured the town, driving up and down the narrow, one-way roads, looking at houses for sale and checking out the neighborhoods. The towering mountain peaks in the backdrop of the city reminded them of quaint towns long ago. The railway ran through the town and behind the visitor's center like those in Old Western movies, leaving them with a certain feeling of nostalgia.

They decided to pack up everything that night, go to Mountain View Church the next morning, and then begin their trek home.

The worship service was contemporary, and the church was not too large. The people made you feel welcome, and the Word was expounded upon.

Brian and Maria felt refreshed as they stood to leave. The pastor and his wife came over and introduced themselves on their way to greet people. They had a pleasant chat and then dismissed themselves to go greet the other visitors.

Chapter Eleven
MYSTERIOUS HAPPENINGS

Barbie twirled the phone in her hand a few minutes, contemplating her decision to share her true feelings with Maria. She was at a pivotal point in their relationship. Either she confessed or continued the distance which only proved to build walls of isolation and more loneliness, while confusing and hurting her best friend.

After a cheery hello, Barbie was prompted to leave a message after the tone. "Hi, friend, I need to meet with you soon. I'm sorry for not responding to your calls and texts. There is no excuse for my behavior. Please, call me."

She fidgeted in her kitchen with the dishes and cleaned out her refrigerator. Her nerves were shot from not getting enough rest and the relentless mind games. She shouted into the air, "This is ridiculous, and I'm sick of it. I rebuke you, Devourer. Get away from me. I'm done with you toying with my emotions. My friend would never reject me. Most of all Jesus will always be there for me. I'm not abandoned by Him, and He will never leave me alone!"

The "*Walk Through the Forest*" ringtone echoed through the kitchen. Barbie grasped her phone and rattled off an apology.

"Slow down, Friend. It's okay. I forgive you. I've missed you. It's good to hear your voice. Are you okay?" Maria replied.

"No, I'm not. The enemy has been messing with my brain, and I gave him full access. I need to see you. Can I come over?"

"Sure. I've an appointment with the investigator at 4. Brian should be home soon, and he can watch Angel."

"Thanks. Be right there." Barbie felt freer than she had in months.

She swung by Bergie's, and picked them up an ice cold pumpkin chai.

Maria almost knocked it out of her hand as she threw her arms around Barbie. "I've missed you!" She exclaimed.

"Oh my goodness, I've missed you too."

"Let's go to the den. Angel is asleep."

"Yummy. This is good. Thanks." Maria sipped the tea in her hand.

"Listen, I need to get this off my chest before I explode. I've been avoiding you. There is no excuse, but there is a reason. Remember when mom died and how abandoned I felt? Since you adopted Angel and became a family, these feelings have risen up in me once again. You are going to think this is silly, but I'm afraid you will too." Barbie sniffled.

"Oh, sweetie. Why would you think that? I'd never abandon you. You are my closest friend. We've been through a lot together."

"I know, but now you've your own family. The night of Angel's party I realized I buried deep desires to belong to someone. The devil chased me around the field with doubt and fear, even though I have the power to kick him out. Please, forgive me."

"You're forgiven. Give me a hug. You'll always be a part of our family. We may be busy, but you're not forgotten. I'm glad you're working and going to school. Maybe you'll meet someone and start your own family."

"I'm pretty independent and stubborn. I don't know if anyone could handle me." They both chuckled.

Maria's cell phone calendar hummed. "Wow, its three o'clock, and Brian isn't home yet. He's late. I need to give him a call. My appointment is at 4."

"I can watch her if he doesn't come home soon."

"Are you sure? She is teething and might be fussy."

"Yeah, we'll be okay. Is your milk in the freezer?"

"Yes, heat it in the warmer. She'll take about six to eight ounces. Burp her after three to four. Her diapers and wipes are in the changing table. Thank you. I'll call Brian while I freshen up."

Maria walked into her closet. "Hey, Honey, where are you?"

Brian exhaled, "Oh no, I forgot your appointment. I'm in the middle of a meeting. There is no way I can make it in time. Can you re-schedule? I'm sorry, Honey."

"It's okay. Barbie is here, and she's going to watch Angel. Touch base with her and let her know how long you will be."

"That's great! Thanks. I should be home by 4:30. Love you."

Maria made a play date with Barbie for the following week and expressed how much they loved her before leaving. She made a mental note to ask her about babysitting during their date times, if her schedule allowed.

Maria met the detective at Black Bear's restaurant. His stern demeanor, top hat and pipe reminded her of Sherlock Holmes. She concealed a chuckle. He interrogated her about the events leading up to and during the phone call. She shared about the visitor that appeared the evening of the call.

"Do you know the description of the person who shot Uncle Ron?" She questioned.

"No. The light above the booth flickered, reveling little, and your uncle said it happened too quickly. He could tell it was a man. He did remember seeing a long overcoat and hat."

Maria gasped. Her face turned white as a sheet. She felt faint.

"Ma'am, are you okay?" He handed her a glass of water.

She reminded herself to breathe. "Yes, the night this all happened, the man at my door wore a trench coat and cap."

"There could be a tie to the two men. It is possible they could have been communicating in between cities. Thanks for not leaving this important detail out. Have you received any more calls or suspicious activity?"

"No," Maria responded.

He stood to shake her hand. "We'll be in touch."

Maria wanted to ask him if he thought they were in any immediate danger, but she didn't know how far the questioning should go because of their predicament with Angel. She wanted to speak with Brian first.

Brian met with Stephanie and her mom before their discharge. They were humbled and grateful for the care received at the hospital. She told him of her plans to continue counseling with Pastor Stroke, join the youth group at a church near their home, and begin family counseling with her step-dad. She decided to give Fred a chance. Her mother's approval shone in her glowing face. The girl's father was arrested for unrelated charges, but was convicted of crimes against his daughter. In addition to his prison time, the courts assigned him to therapy.

Stephanie explained, "Our relationship may never be restored, but at least I know he isn't hurting another child and getting the help he needs. Thank you for everything you did for me." She stood and hugged Brian. "I hope we can remain friends."

"Yes, I would like that."

Brian's phone rang as he walked them out. It was Barbie.

"Yes, I'm on my way."

Maria and Brian drove up at the same time. She pulled into the driveway first.

"Wow, your appointment went quickly. How did it go?" Brian quipped.

"A little scary; I found out the man who shot Ron wore a coat and hat like our circus visitor."

"Hmmm. They were miles apart though."

Barbie heard them and opened the door. Angel rested on her right hip.

"This is the best baby ever! I love her! You can count me as your official babysitter!" She exclaimed.

"It's funny you mention that because we've been discussing getting a weekly sitter." Maria related.

"Awesome, but for now I gotta book. I've class in an hour. Call me next week. I will answer or phone you back, I promise. Love you." She hugged them and kissed Angel.

Brian took the baby and Maria started dinner.

He hollered from the living room, "Don't cook. Let's go out, please."

"Babe, we ate out last night. Shouldn't we be saving our money for our move to Flagstaff?" She teased.

His phone buzzed. "Hello. Let me ask Maria."

He walked in the kitchen. "Hon, Larry wants to bring his girlfriend by to meet us. Are you okay with that?"

"I guess. Ask if they want to eat supper with us?"

Brian walked away, chatting intently. After his discussion ended, he came back into the room exclaiming, "Yes! They will be here at 6:30. Do you need me to help you?"

He pulled Angel's bouncy into the kitchen and placed towels around her back to stabilize her. She smacked her small hands against the buttons and cackled gleefully.

"You can chop the veggies for a salad and make sweet iced tea. Use the honey, please. What makes this girl different from the other ladies he has dated?"

"I think his other relationships have been shallow, probably because of his fear of commitment. Thanks, Babe, for being open to meeting with them. From what Larry says, Adaline is not a flighty personality; she is strong and sure of herself. Her passion is compassion. She is a coordinator of family affairs at New Life's Center for Homeless Families. I know they've struggled in their relationship. Maybe we can be a positive influence on them since I'm such an awesome husband." He winked at her.

"Oh and what am I, chopped liver? I'm actually looking forward to meeting her." She tickled his sides.

Angel got mad because the music quit on her dangling toy. Her dad laughed and poked it with his toe. She instantly cheered up.

Larry and Adaline arrived promptly at 6:30. Her medium-built frame tucked perfectly under his long arm as it draped over her shoulder. She wore a cute skort and aqua tank top, which brought out her dazzling eyes. They enjoyed a light-hearted dinner and played a strategic dominoes game called Chicken Foot. Then the women retreated to the nursery in an effort to feed Angel and have some girl conversation.

Brian and Larry cleaned up the kitchen.

"Isn't she the best? She's got me considering going to mechanical school to learn how to repair trucks," Larry said.

"Wow. You said you would never go to college. I think it's great. You are intelligent and good with your hands."

"She's pushing me, and we still fight a lot, but I love her. I met with Pastor Stroke and he is counseling me. I told him we would commit to couples' sessions before we get married."

"Married! You're serious." Brian high-fived him.

"Totally! I think we'll be good together. I calm her strong New York personality, and she demands more from me than anyone ever has. She's much stronger in her faith, but I'm growing."

'I'm proud of you, Bro."

"Thanks to you! If it hadn't been for you, I would've walked away the night we met to shoot pool."

"But you didn't. It'll be hard work. Marriage isn't for wimps. It's for real men who fight for what they want."

"I believe I can do it. I'm going to ask her to marry me on her birthday, November 18, but I need your help to make it special. You are good with this kind of stuff. When it gets closer, I'll meet with you to get ideas, okay?"

"Yes, and I'm sure Maria will have great input too."

" Thanks for being there for me," Larry replied.

Maria found this new-found friend to be intriguing. Her intelligent, fun and caring personality pleased her, plus Angel cuddled with her right away. The child seemed relaxed in her presence. She envied her soft brunette curls that hung loosely across her shoulders. The children teased Maria unmercifully as a child, calling her "carrot top" and pulling at her long locks.

"Do you have any children? You seem like a natural," Maria commented.

"No, but I'm the oldest of five siblings. I've been a second mom as long as I can remember."

Larry popped his head in the room. "Hey Babe, I've got a job at 6 am; we should probably get going."

Brian and Maria walked them out into the dusty windblown night.

Adaline hugged them, "Thank you for the delightful evening. I hope we can visit again soon."

Chapter Twelve
VISIT TO OASIS

The next few months whizzed by. At six months old, Angel was trying to pull herself up on all fours and crawl, getting stronger and more playful every day. She was eating homemade baby food and beginning to take sips from a sippy cup. Her breastfeeding decreased significantly, and Maria was healing nicely.

Uncle Ron recovered and was now in a rehabilitation hospital. He asked Brian and Maria to visit him, but with Brian's busy schedule at work, it was hard to get more time off.

Ron wrote a letter explaining the epiphany he experienced. He apologized for his harsh words and treatment at their last hospital encounter. His life changed a lot since the robbery, and he didn't want to be an alcoholic anymore. He wanted to be someone his daughter would have been proud of. The hospital was helping him, and he talked to the chaplain on a day-to-day basis. They were elated to hear about the changes in him and planned a trip in April to visit him.

Maria's dad was responding well to his treatments at the Oasis of Hope hospital. She flew there for the last three days of his treatment; Barbie stayed with Angel while Brian worked. Her classes ended and work slowed down enough for her to take a short leave.

Aaron was on a strict diet to which they all adhered to when eating with him. The hospital staff was exceptional, but they were definitely on their own time schedule compared to the busyness of the city in which they lived. It was a special time of reprieve with her mom and dad despite the circumstances. Eula and Maria took long walks down by the sandy ocean shore. They watched the people collect small sand crabs. The culture afforded them the opportunity to steam the small sea-life for their eating pleasure.

Maria and her mom visited a historic landmark, Hotel del Coronado, with its red roofs, upscale restaurants, and inviting pools. The gardens there held a mysterious ambiance. The roses smelled like sweet perfume, delicate in beauty, and the thorns reminded Maria of hidden dangers with their razor sharpness piercing her skin as she pulled the blossoms close to sniff. Birds of Paradise stood gracious and tall behind the outer wall. Their colors of vibrant orange and red, back-dropped against luscious green foliage, part of the leaves curled in a way to reveal that for which they were named, a bird with its feathers flying upward like a male's mating call in its full glory. The spider daisies drew her to their irresistible delicacy, petals thinly interwoven with deep rustic yellow stripes. The live blooms bursting forth in intensity pushing the lifeless blossoms away reminded her of the ebb of life.

Angel fussed a lot the first two days Maria was gone, but when Barbie put the phone up to her ear, her mommy's voice soothed her.

"I miss her terribly. I'm never leaving her again!" Maria would confess to her friend.

The long walks by the ocean helped ease her troubled mind. She would sit on the balcony of her parent's hospital room, and they would talk of home, the future, and Skype Brian and Angel.

One night Aaron came out with a hot tea in his hand and sat down with a serious look on his face. "I know you ladies don't want to talk about this, but we must. Maria. Your mom and I have made arrangements at Mariposa Gardens. The staff is respectful, courteous and compassionate. It's a lovely place with rose gardens, memory plaques, and streams of water. I want to be cremated, and your mother can setup a special commemorative inscription with a picture in the gardens or on a rock in the water in my memory."

"Dad, you are looking much better. Your color is returning, and you're stronger." Maria sternly replied. "The doctors seem hopeful too."

Deliberately, he continued, ignoring her statement, "Whether now's my time or later, your mom will be taken care of. I have setup an educational fund for Angel; if by chance you don't need it, give it to a child who does. Samantha at the mortuary has written down my exact specifications on how I want my ceremony, music, and my final instructions for them and my family. One more thing, I know you and Brian haven't mentioned adopting other children, but we feel you should. There are many youngsters who need a loving home. You are good parents. I've opened an account to help you with the expenses. Your mom's name is on the savings plan, and she will have a say in how the money is used. I know you two will work it out together and do what's best." He started coughing as he always did when he talked too much. He spit up blood and tried to hide it in a napkin, but Maria and Eula saw it.

"I'm calling Dr. Contreras," Eula shrieked as she rose from her chair.

Aaron held his hand up, "No! He said it could still happen at times. I'm okay. Sit down, Honey." He compassionately looked at her. "I'm not through yet." He looked Maria dead square in her eyes. "I love you. You are my child. Be strong and courageous. Do not fear. Help your mother. You are the best daughter a man could ever have. I want you to know I'm proud of the woman you are. Thank you for leading your mom and me to Jesus." Then he got up, kissed her on the head, and steadied himself against the chair. Eula stood to help him, and he leaned hard into her. She helped him back into his bed.

Maria clasped her face in her hands and wept quietly, letting her requests be known to God. "Lord, please don't let my daddy die, not now."

Alice Voyles and her husband, Melvin, have lived in Arizona for twenty years. Alice enjoys writing, sharing her desire for people to pursue their dreams through speaking and teaching, playing with her grandchildren, and hiking. After the inspiration of a high school creative writing course, she pursued her passion by writing children's books and short stories. Alice hopes her writings will motivate readers to search for meaning beyond their circumstances, to find springs in the barren regions of life. Alice's hope is that the creative writings within these pages bring healing to the wounds of your soul.

a Book's Mind

Whether you want to purchase bulk copies of
Life's Oasis
or buy another book for a friend, get it now at:
www.abooksmart.com

If you have a book that you would like to publish,
contact Jenene Scott, Publisher, at A Book's Mind:
jenene@abooksmind.com.

www.abooksmind.com